MW00917431

Alec: A Scottish Outlaw

Highland Outlaws, Volume 4

Lily Baldwin

Published by Lily Baldwin, 2021.

ALEC: A SCOTTISH OUTLAW

First edition. March 18, 2021.

Written by Lily Baldwin.

To my all my Angels

Chapter One
London, England
1302

Joanie Picard swept the silk robe from her mistress's shoulders. Diana Faintree, a famed London beauty and singer, dressed in rich fabrics and vibrant hues, but she was as common as Joanie — both born to poverty, both fighting each day to survive.

Frowning, Joanie lifted Diana's arm and inspected the red, horizontal stripes marring the fine skin below her shoulder — thick, evenly spaced markings left behind like a cruel keepsake from their master's biting fingers.

"Leave them for now," Diana said, keeping her eyes averted. "The morning grows old, like me, and we've still much to do."

Joanie nodded and reached for the pumice stone. She ran her thumb across the abrasive, porous surface and winced. She loathed what would happen next. Glancing at Diana's weary face, she couldn't help but suggest, "Where it isn't bruised, your skin is already so soft. Why don't we skip the stone?"

"You already know my answer," Diana said, her lips curving in a soft smile. "But I love you for trying. Go on," she said, the last words at a whisper.

Joanie took a deep breath. Starting at Diana's toes and working her way up her long leg, she set to work scouring Diana's skin with the stone in small, circular motions.

"You're too gentle," Diana said, gritting her teeth.

Joanie looked up at her. "You are not well. I do not wish to hurt you."

A forced smile stretched Diana's lips wide. "I'm fine. You worry too much." She shifted her gaze away from Joanie's. "Do it right."

Joanie looked longingly at the window and imagined throwing back the shutters and hurling the hateful stone beyond the palace walls. She tightened her grip around it. If only she could crush it to dust, but then her fingers fell slack, the stone neither soaring through the air nor crumbling to the floor. It filled her palm, and it was just as well — Diana would only procure another for her routine ablutions. For nearly five years, Joanie had served as Diana's maid, and in all that time, they had never skipped her weekly rigorous beauty treatments — despite any new bruises received at the hands of their master or her failing health. Pressing her lips together in a grim line, Joanie gripped Diana's thigh and continued scrubbing until her skin shone red.

"Have the others faded?" Diana asked when Joanie scooted on her knees around to Diana's backside. Angry bruises in varying shades of red, brown, and yellow marred her back, buttock, and thighs.

"A little," Joanie said, setting the stone aside. She reached into a basket of tins and pouches filled with various creams, ointments and powders. She took up the comfrey ointment. She scooped a great dollop of the greasy balm, then dotted it over Diana's bruises before gently rubbing the soothing ointment into her skin.

"Geoffrey was in a particularly foul mood last night," Diana murmured.

Joanie didn't respond. When was the master not in a foul mood?

"Look at me," Diana entreated her.

Joanie did as she was bidden.

"Your interference must stop. He was vexed with me, not you. He never would have touched you had you not stepped in front of me."

Joanie lowered her gaze and continued applying the balm. "You cannot ask me to stand idly by while he beats you." Then she stopped rubbing and looked up, locking eyes with her mistress once more. "I will not do that," she avowed through gritted teeth.

"Joanie—" Diana began, but then a deep, wet cough stole her words and her breath. Her whole body jerked as if under attack from the inside out. Joanie jumped to her feet and wrapped her arms around Diana to support her. When at last the coughing ceased and Diana caught her breath, she wiped at her eyes and smiled weakly at Joanie. "Thank you," she rasped. Then she slowly reached out a trembling hand toward the hem of Joanie's tunic. "How do your gifts from our master fare?"

Diana's weakened state broke Joanie's heart. Shaking her head, she implored, "Do not worry for me. Mine always heal quickly." Then she scooped more salve and spread it over the fresh fingerprints on Diana's arm. "You must save your strength. I'm nearly finished, then you can get into the bath." Joanie glanced at the tub in front of the hearth. Steam curled in ghostly ribbons from the oily surface.

"It will do me good. I know it will," Diana said. Then she smiled at Joanie. "I see your worry. It is etched on your dear face, visible even beneath the grime you refuse to let me help scrub away. This cough will pass."

Joanie frowned. "I'm only permitted to bathe once a fortnight. I do not fancy being clean enough to attract the master's fury." She looked away before continuing in a gentle voice. "The cough is persisting this time."

"I know," Diana said.

The truth hung in the air between them for a moment like an ominous cloud, but Diana chased the storm away with her bright voice. "Anyway, you've always managed to cure me in the past."

Joanie scanned Diana's body. Unlike Joanie, who was shorter and slimly built, Diana had always enjoyed lush, full curves that drove men wild. But her cough had worsened over the last fortnight, and her body had begun to waste away. Joanie fought to keep her concern from showing. "The next time Simon checks in on us, I am going to have him bring up another meal for you."

Diana shook her head. "I am still full after breaking our fast. I couldn't possibly eat again so soon."

"You will if you want to be stronger." Joanie wrapped her arm around Diana's waist. "Let me help you into the bath."

"Wait," Diana said.

Joanie stood still and looked at her expectantly.

"Could I have a mirror?"

Nodding, Joanie reached for the small, gilded compact on Diana's bedside table and gave it to her. Diana held the glass up, scrutinizing her features. She pulled at the skin beneath her eyes and the soft lines framing her mouth. "I'm a disgrace."

Joanie glanced up from the beauty mask she was mixing. "You are the most beautiful woman in London."

Diana's expression softened. "And you are forever my champion, even when I battle myself." Then she turned back and continued studying her own reflection. "I was the most beautiful woman in London. But age is robbing me of the title all too soon. That is what happens when you turn thirty."

"You are not yet thirty."

"No, but I am eight and twenty." Diana frowned again at what she saw in the mirror. "I may as well be a hundred." With a sigh, she set the compact down. "At nineteen, Joanie, you can hardly understand." Then she slid the robe from her shoulders and continued in a brighter voice. "Have you mixed the porridge mask?"

Joanie nodded, relieved for the change in subject. "Let's get you into the tub first." She helped Diana step into the steamy water. Joanie had poured liberal amounts of chamomile and lavender oils into the bath to soothe Diana's bruises, and the heady scents wafted off the surface as the water rose to make room for her battle-wearied body. Diana groaned when she eased back. Joanie smiled, realizing by the contented look on Diana's face that she voiced her pleasure rather than discomfort. Picking up the clay dish filled with a mixture of roughly cut oats and heavy cream, she smoothed a thick layer onto Diana's upturned face.

"What will I do when my looks finally go, Joanie? Geoffrey will turn me out."

Flashes of the master's hulking fists and cruel eyes raced through Joanie's mind, chasing her smile away. "Would that really be so awful?"

Diana opened her eyes and gave Joanie a hard look. "There are worse pains than fist or lash. Hunger. Cold. They are the real demons." Her face softened. "I know you have suffered greatly at the hands of your masters and your father before he sold you. But Joanie..." Diana shifted her gaze but not before Joanie saw the sudden sheen of unshed tears in her eyes. "You have never known true hunger or cold. Don't ever fool yourself into thinking you'd be better off somewhere else." Diana turned back to look at her. Her tears were gone, and her eyes shone clear and strong. "Our master is rich." She lifted a dripping hand from the water and made a sweeping gesture. "Look at this room, at the warm bed we share and in the king's palace, no less. We are the lucky ones, Joanie. Out there, the streets are full of people a breath away from death who would withstand any number of abuses to have what we possess."

Joanie shifted her gaze away from Diana's stubborn resolve wondering whether her friend was right. Were they, indeed, better off with the master? More than once, she had asked Diana to run away with her, but she had always refused and warned Joanie not to dream beyond survival. But Joanie couldn't help wondering — was it really a choice between beatings and abuse or starvation and freezing? Couldn't there be another life for them — one without the constant threat of pain or death? She dipped her finger into a pot of honey and willow oil and worked the mixture into her hands before gently weaving her fingers through Diana's wet hair.

Her mistress sighed as her elbows came up on the sides of the tub. "That feels so good. I've had such a headache."

"You should have told me sooner," Joanie scolded. Then she cupped her hand and closed her eyes, imagining a ball of light at rest in her palm. Curving her palm over Diana's forehead, she closed her eyes and took deep, slow breaths and imagined heat radiated from the light in her hand, surrounding Diana's pain. She stayed there for a long while, confronting the darkness with her healing touch.

Diana sighed. "You're an angel."

Joanie opened her eyes. "You don't believe in angels."

Diana smiled. "For the moment I do."

"Then the pain is gone. Good," Joanie said, happy to have alleviated at least a little of Diana's suffering. She wrapped her fingers around the handle of a small copper pot and dipped it in the bath water to rinse Diana's hair. But a sharp rapping on the door startled her, and she dropped the handle, losing the pot beneath the surface. Jumping to her feet, she came around the screen that shielded her mistress, just as a barrel-chested man of great height with thinning brown hair, a neatly trimmed beard, and a red nose from too much ale walked into the room.

Joanie expelled the breath she'd been holding. "Thank God it's you, Simon."

Simon was their master's manservant. To most people, he was gruff and hard — full of bite, but beneath his coarse surface, hid a gentleness only shown to Diana and thus to Joanie by default.

He motioned toward the screen and mouthed the words, how is she?

Lips pressed into a thin line, Joanie only shook her head in answer.

"Damn it," Simon cursed.

Straightaway, Joanie's heart started to pound. "What is it?" she whispered. Then she heard the water slosh and knew Diana had sat up.

"Is that Simon? Is something wrong?"

His powerful shoulders sagged. Sad eyes met Joanie's. "Geoffrey wants you in the hall tonight," he said loud enough for Diana to hear.

Joanie's eyes widened. "But tonight is Anabel's night to entertain."

Simon put his hand up, silencing her protest. "She doesn't have to perform, but he insists she attend the evening meal and stay for the entertainment following."

Water sloshed again. Joanie hurried around the screen.

"I must get out," Diana said, struggling to stand. "My hair will never dry in time. And my gown still needs freshening. Joanie, what will I — "

Joanie's chest tightened at the sound of Diana's sudden cough, which racked her shoulders. She white-knuckled the sides of the tub to keep her face out of the water. Joanie dropped to her knees and wrapped her arms around Diana, supporting her. Wet hacking subsided into strangled wheezing and finally gasps for air. When, at last, the cough ran its course, Diana turned her face up to look at Joanie. Joanie's heart ached at the sight of her red, tear-streaked face and wide, terrified green eyes. She trembled in Joanie's arms. "Let's get you dry," Joanie said, her voice soothing. She helped Diana step from the tub, then dried her off and swept her robe around her shoulders.

"She is decent," Joanie called. "I need your help, Simon."

Simon appeared an instant later, his face drained of color. He scooped Diana into his arms.

"Simon's got you." Joanie heard him whisper.

Joanie hurried around the screen and rushed to the bed, grabbing pillows and blankets, which she then arranged near the hearth. "Lay her down and fan her hair out so it dries," she told him. Then she hurried to the table and seized a small pouch of mustard powder from a basket, which she quickly mixed with flour, warm water from the bath, and vinegar. Then she knelt beside Diana.

"Make sure she is ready," Simon said to Joanie.

She nodded and carried on mixing the mustard paste while she watched Simon gently stroke Diana's cheek with the back of his fingers. Then he stood and strode from the room.

Joanie gave the thick paste a final stir. Then she opened Diana's robe, exposing her chest.

"No," her mistress said, waving her away. "I will stink. Just lay your hands on me. Your touch alone has healed me before."

Joanie shook her head. "I promise it will wash away, and lavender oil will hide the smell. It will hopefully stave off another attack for some time, allowing you to regain your strength."

Diana closed her eyes. "Fine, but just a thin layer. Then you must ready my face."

Joanie thickly coated her chest with the foul-smelling mixture, despite her protests. Then she set to work combining a fine white powder with vinegar and egg white. Using a bristly brush, she made sweeping strokes across Diana's mottled complexion, until it gleamed white. Then she dabbed soft pink rouge on the apples of both her cheeks. Taking a step back, she scrutinized Diana's appearance.

Her brows were plucked to thin, pale crescent moons. Her hair cascaded across the floor in thick waves and shone almost white, it was so blond. She did not require onion skins or lemon juice to lighten the color, unlike so many of the women at court, whose dull hair looked more orange than blond as a result of their efforts. Everything about Diana was naturally built to seduce, from her curvy figure to the throaty tone of her voice. And when she sang, men stopped and stared with hungry eyes. Joanie chewed her lip as she impatiently waited for her mistress's hair to dry.

Simon returned a few hours later. "That will have to do," he said, his voice strained. "The hour for supper is almost here."

He gently helped Diana to her feet and wrapped his arm around her waist.

"No," she said, not unkindly. "I can manage."

Tears stung Joanie's eyes as she watched her mistress gracefully cross the room to sit at her table where a gilded mirror reflected her ethereal beauty. Knowing the pain she must have felt tore at Joanie's heart, although Diana let none of it show.

Joanie crossed the room and took hold of Diana's comb and pulled her long bangs back to lengthen her brow. When her hair was pinned in place, she arranged the sides so that golden waves spilled over Diana's shoulders past her waist. Then she helped her dress.

"Will Geoffrey approve?" Diana asked nervously, smoothing her hands over the intricately embroidered bodice of her pale green tunic.

Joanie doubted anyone could ever fully meet with the master's approval. Still, Diana's beauty was unmatched regardless of the passing of time. "You look stunning. Mind you do not overdo it. Hold your tongue so that you do not strain your voice. Remember, you have to perform tomorrow night."

Diana nodded. "I will remember. I am hoping to get away as soon as I can."

Simon filled the doorway with his large frame. "It is time."

Diana stood and kissed Joanie on the cheek before she crossed the room and left on Simon's arm.

Joanie stared at the closed door for a moment. Then she numbly turned and stiffly sat in Diana's seat and looked at her own reflection in the mirror. Her greasy black hair hung limply past her shoulders. Her brown eyes looked back at her, dull, void of joy and life. As ever, her face was hidden beneath a layer of dirt and grime. Her master didn't allow her a bath of her own. None of the ointments, oils, or perfumes on the table were for her use. She wore the same worn, tattered tunic every day. Once a fortnight, she was permitted to wash herself and her clothing in Diana's used bath water. Not for her own benefit or health, but only so that the master didn't have to smell her. Geoffrey Mercer's cruel, twisted smiled came to the fore of her mind. Unlike Diana, she at least did not have to face him every day. Diana went to his room to perform her duties as leman. But whenever he did enter their room, it always meant the worst. The sound of his footfalls and that of his guard, who followed him everywhere, would echo through the stone corridor like thunder. A shiver shot up Joanie's spine just thinking about the din of their master's approach. She closed her eyes. Her heart pounded. Her breaths came short.

"Help us," she whispered to no one, for who would hear the pleas of someone as insignificant as she?

Joanie whirled away from the sad creature she saw in the mirror, stood up and started to clean the room. She would keep moving, keep doing, despite her fatigue. She couldn't stop. If she did, she would be forced to face the truth about Diana who was her one light in the dark. Her beloved mistress's health had been failing for months, but she had managed with Joanie's help. Still, the past fortnight had taken its toll.

"No," she said out loud and fought back her tears.

After all, Diana continued to fight. She carried on, bravely surviving, and so would Joanie. That is what life had always been. It was what life would always be — a desperate fight for survival.

Chapter Two

A frigid gust of winter's chill strikes Alec's face while he hovers in the night air far above the city of London. Orange torch fire flickers like stars across the shadowy cityscape. Silence engulfs him, soothes him. He is cold and alone, but his mind is all his own, not burdened by other's emotions or visions of tragedies yet to come. He is out of reach, flying above the human pain revealed to his seer's eyes.

But then he feels a tug from below.

"No," he says, his voice flat.

He turns onto his back and stares up at stars, distant guardians, but of whom or what? He once believed they were angels, but he stopped believing in angels long ago. Too many people suffered needlessly for angels to be real. He covers his face with his hands. Again, he feels a pull in his heart, a soul pleading for his. His hands fall away. Large snowflakes cascade and dance, whirling in swirling circles from a now starless sky. He sighs and spreads his arms wide, like a bird, and drifts down. The vague city shapes become defined — shacks, warehouses, churches, fortresses, docks, riverboats, and bridges.

Then he sees her.

She is standing on a narrow, wrought iron bridge, guarded by two lions, their faces watchful and regal. But those stone sentinels cannot save her, only he can. Her shoulders tensely hug her ears as she pulls the folds of her tattered cloak tighter against the wintry night. Fear and pain coil like writhing snakes around her heart. His long arm extends, reaching down to her, comforting her. Her *wide dark eyes brim full of tears. Heartbroken. Hungry. Cold. Her pleas ride upon the whirling snow until they reach his ear in a whisper. "Help us."*

He descends, swooping down, stopping a breath away from her face. He meets her gaze.

"Alec," she whispers, a puff of icy breath leaving her lips.

Alec MacVie sat up with a start, his thin wool blanket pooling around his hips. His heart pounded in his ears, along with the dizzying accompaniment of another's heartbeat, her heartbeat. He threw back the covers, swung his legs over the side of the bed, and rested his head in his hands. A flash of cold lingering from the wintry dream passed over him, chilling his naked body. Shivering, he wrapped his fingers around the shard of stone, nearly purple in color, which hung from a long, leather strip around his neck. Heat emanated from the stone. He closed his eyes, inviting the warmth to imbue his body. The chill fled, but whoever she was, the poor, heartbroken lass on the bridge, her pain still gripped his soul. Her fear quickened his own pulse. He took a deep, slow breath and willed it all to cease. Slowly, everything drained away, leaving the hollowness inside him to which he had grown accustomed.

He crossed to stand in front of the hearth. Orange embers glowed in the darkness. Closing his eyes, he again saw her pale face and heard his name on her lips. Still staring at smoldering ash, he backed up a few steps and sat in the high-backed chair. The stone shard he wore now felt cool against his skin. He wrapped his fingers around it, wondering about the secrets it held — secrets kept even from his divining gaze.

The stone had come to him by the Abbot Matthew of Haddington Abbey. The Abbot led a secret network of Scottish rebels to which Alec and his brothers belonged. Before set-ting out on his latest assignment, the abbot had given Alec the shard and told him that it contained a secret he hoped Alec could reveal — a secret of great importance to the cause.

"Somehow, Scotland's fate is tied to this broken shard," the abbot had told him.

For months now, he had pondered the stone, but it had re-mained quiet, soulless; that is, until three nights ago, when he started dreaming about the lass on the bridge. Suddenly, the stone had allusively revealed itself, warming when her heart-beat accompanied his own. This was the third time he had dreamt of her, and now the third time he had felt the stone's fire. But who was she? And what did it all mean?

He raked both hands through his hair, as he glanced about the room. One thing he knew for certain — the answers were not hiding there in his chamber. He needed to get out. Letting the cool stone fall against his chest, he stood and crossed to his wardrobe and grabbed a pair of hose. He pulled them on, set-tling the waistband low on his hips. Then he yanked on a black tunic, which he belted at his waist. Within his tall boots, he hid a dagger. And after securing his sword to his back, he swept a thick, black cloak over his shoulders and headed toward the door.

Stepping into the hallway, he shut the door and locked it before setting out down the corridor, which was illuminated by candlelight. At the end of the hallway, he turned onto a land-ing. His eyes, as always, were drawn straight ahead where a mas-sive shield bore the King of England's coat of arms. The large display served as Alec's daily reminder that he was, indeed, living in King Edward's palace in London — or at least a wealthy English merchant named Randolph Tweed was.

For several months now, Alec had been living under the alias of Randolph Tweed, spying on the English court by order of Abbot Matthew. But in all that time, King Edward had not actually been in residence. He had moved his household to York where he readied his army for war, bringing a six-month truce with Scotland soon to an end. In his absence, he had left his palace in London in the less than capable hands of a man named John Bigge. The keepership was John's according to hereditary laws, but as keeper, he had done little to preserve courtly order. Rather, his salacious appetites had invited all manner of sinners to court. He had even tempted the monks in the adjacent abbey to partake in his unholy revelries. In fact, it was rumors of the monks' debauchery that compelled the abbot to send one of his secret rebels to the palace in the first place, and it was no surprise that he assigned Alec to the task.

Of all the secret rebels in Scotland, Alec was particularly adept as a spy, owing to gifts that had both served and plagued him his entire life. In the simplest of terms, Alec possessed the Sight. He could feel what another person was feeling, and if he laid his hand on someone, he saw into their soul — their fears, pains, sorrows, and desires. When it served him to be charming, no one could resist him. He could sense a person's response to him, guiding his word and deed. They invariably told him exactly what they needed to hear. Lies could never fool him. Detecting deception came as naturally to him as breathing. More than that, he had visions, dreams that revealed need or what loomed in the future — like his dream of the heartbroken lass on the bridge.

When he was not pretending to be someone else, he chose to isolate his thoughts, to buffer and block out the voices. Over the years, he had learned to erect walls around his senses, shielding his heart and mind from the continuous barrage of human emotion. As a result, most thought him cold-hearted ... a hard man. And whether true or not, he did nothing to change their minds. He preferred to keep people at a distance. They were all too human, too quick to distrust and to assume the worst of themselves and others. The inner workings of another's mind were seldom uplifting. Most of the time, it was like walking through a nightmare of despair, and the king's palace was no different. The keeper had amassed a collection of companions with the vilest of hearts, bent only on baseless pleasures.

He knew not the hour as he approached the great hall, but he would be able to judge the time depending on how drunk the revelers were. He closed his eyes, steeling his strength against the assault of emotion as he pulled open the large double doors and walked headlong into the large room. Piercing laughter and battling voices echoed off the vaulted ceilings. Raucous men salivated after dancers who languidly moved among the tables, undulating their hips in layers of sheer silk. Barmaids busily skirted around the dancers, filling greedy fists with large tankards of ale at a speed that meant the night was still young.

He took a step forward just as one of the dancers twirled away from groping hands straight into Alec. Her hands splayed across his chest as she looked up to meet his eyes. Flashes of her life came unbidden to his mind; a little girl loved and treasured, a father lost at sea, a mother with no place to turn, a life torn asunder, a beautiful young woman alone.

"I'm sorry," she said, a sensual smile curving her lips. But then her eyes narrowed on his, and her smiled vanished. She dropped her hands to her sides. "Randolph," she said, surprise and trepidation lacing her voice.

He held her gaze but revealed none of what he'd glimpsed of her. Nor did he acknowledge her distrust of him. The dancers and serving maids were all afraid of him. They had seen his black eyes and cool facade and assumed the worst of him. Rumors abounded of his cruel sexual appetites, although he had never taken any one of them to his bed. Still, he did naught to dispel the rumors as it kept them away. Eyes now wide, the dancer turned and darted away from him.

He cleared her from his thoughts, emptying his heart and mind, choosing numbness over the lust, greed, hunger, and fear, which pulsed through the room and fought to enter him. Only snatches of emotion made it past. But then an ache so soft and pure, cut through the rest, overtaking all his defenses. Pain accompanied by truth rang out, even in its gentleness, above the din of desperation. His eyes fell on a woman he had seen many times before. Her name was Diana. Her flaxen hair trailed the ground where she sat, and her green eyes shone with mirth and delight. She was an actress without equal. Those surrounding her, her many admirers, could never have guessed the pain she was in. Only Alec knew that which even she might not have known herself. She was dying. He could feel the struggle for life in her waning heartbeat, but something or someone was keeping her alive. He looked at the large, detestable man at her side and knew he was not the reason behind her strength.

"Randolph," a voice called out.

Alec turned and locked eyes with the keeper. John's thick black hair curled close to his scalp. He had just celebrated his fortieth year with all the pomp of a true royal despite the humbleness of his birth. He was neither lord nor knight, but he carried himself as though he were king. He raised his tankard as Alec approached. "Randolph, I've not seen you for days." His small, brown eyes darted left then right before he continued in a quiet voice. "Have you any news?"

Alec, of course, knew what John sought. Unbeknownst to anyone, from the very beginning, Alec had been pitting John's companions against one another, mostly merchants and some lesser nobles, inciting conflict among the ranks. Then he revealed the subsequent deceptions and misgivings to John, earning his unquestioned trust. In turn, John's approval protected him from the others, that and his own stony demeanor.

"I've nothing to report," Alec said, his face and voice impassive.

John nodded, then his eyes left Alec's as one of the dancers enticed him with the gentle sway of her hips. The keeper grabbed her. Alec looked away. Hazy drunkenness blurred John's emotions, but he had at least what he thought he wanted — a tankard in one hand and a woman on his lap who was not his wife. Alec resisted the urge to shake his head in disgust as John palmed the dancer's breast. He turned and started to walk away. He had to get out of there.

"Will you not join us?" the keeper called.

Alec glanced back. "I've some business to take care of."

"Some evening you must bring your business here so that we might meet her," the keeper called after him, laughing.

With a cool nod, Alec turned away from John's greed. Ignoring the stares as he passed through the revelers, he stepped out into the courtyard and welcomed the sting of icy wind. The city awaited him, and perhaps this night he would find what kept him in London — the lass from his dreams.

Chapter Three

A lec crossed the king's bridge and dropped a coin into the waiting hand of the river man. Then he stepped into the long, short-sided boat, easily absorbing the choppy waves in his stance as he leisurely took his seat. The MacVie men had grown up in Berwick Upon Tweed, the former Scottish center for commerce and trade. Once upon a time, they had been sailors and dock laborers. But those days had become only distant memory.

Seven years ago, King Edward of England attacked the once prosperous Scottish port, mercilessly massacring thousands of its residents, men, women, and children, even clergy members had not been spared. Now, Berwick was a shadow of its former glory, becoming nothing more than a military post for Edward's burgeoning forces. Alec had been within the city limits when Edward attacked and had witnessed the brutal slaughter with his own eyes. He had only narrowly escaped being one of the many lost souls to have been buried in one of the mass graves dug right into the city streets. The tortured cries of the dying came unbidden to his mind. He fought to silence the pain and death, which continued to haunt him every day of his life.

The black hood of the river man's cloak hung low over his head, shielding his face from the icy wind that blasted down the river. Without once peering out from beneath the folds of black fabric, he rowed the skiff to the other side of the Thames. "This is my last trip until dawn," he rasped, still not looking up.

Alec could feel his fatigue, but more than that, indifferent to the world around him.

Alec tossed an extra coin at the man's feet before silently pulling himself with ease onto the pier. Then without a backward glance, he walked to the end of the dock. The dirt roads and storehouses in front of him were shrouded in shadow. Soft, wet snowflakes floated down from the starless sky, settling on the hard ground at his feet. He breathed in the sharp, clean air and glanced about, not yet knowing where to start his search. For the past three nights, ever since he had first dreamed of the girl with haunting eyes, he had searched the city for the wrought iron bridge, but to no avail. This night he hoped would be different.

He turned about, looking down each path. Then the answer came to him. Something had compelled him down a narrow dirt road that hugged a long row of shabby clay and thatch huts facing the Thames. Wagons had cut deep grooves in the mud during the day, but when the sun set, inviting night's chill, the mud froze, making the road uneven beneath his feet. He stopped short. A sense of urgency struck him. Then the flash of a sweet, young woman's face came to the fore of his mind. Her brow was pinched with worry. About her shoulders hung a pink tattered shawl, and she stared at the door, willing it to open. A breath later, the vision was gone, but the urgency remained.

His eyes narrowed on the road as he quickened his pace. Turning the corner, he spotted an older woman with long, brown hair splashed with silver; a full figure revealed by her low-cut bodice; and blue eyes, not unlike the girl's eyes in his vision, but for the streaks of charcoal running down her cheeks.

The woman took a bottle to her lips. Dark red wine dribbled down her chin and rolled over her ample display. In her other hand, she clutched a knife, the tip of which she pressed to a plump man's fleshy neck. He lay unmoving on the ground, his finely made tunic dotted with snowflakes. However, his stillness could not be blamed on fear of his throat being slit. Too much ale had rendered him unconscious.

Alec surged forward and grabbed the woman's arm. Instantly, he saw in his mind's eye the same woman, her hair swept high and her face neatly made up, sitting with the now unconscious man in a tavern. She plied him with drink while whispering salacious promises in his ear. Her true intentions could not hide from Alec. She had planned to seduce the man, rob him, then leave him to the mercy of the cruel streets and frosty cold.

"Put down the knife."

The woman gasped when she felt a strong hand close around her arm. Two men with exceptionally long black hair and cold, black eyes hovered over her. She blinked and the two faces became one. "Who are you?" she snapped, jerking her arm free. "I don't know you. What do you want?"

She trembled beneath his intense gaze. His eyes bored into hers, not cold anymore but searching. He reached for her arm again, this time holding her in a vice-like grip. She tried to yank free, but he only squeezed harder. Then he wrenched the knife from her hand and tossed it toward the Thames. The slight splash a moment later told her that her hard-earned weapon was lost forever.

"That was mine," she snarled.

He leaned closer, his black eyes trapping her gaze, stealing away her other protests before they could even be uttered. She drew a sharp breath when he gently touched the top of her hand. Then his fingers wove through hers, and suddenly a heat, rich and warm, surrounded her, blocking out the cold. She felt as if she stood near a blazing hearth. Her knees trembled. Her eyes wanted to close, but his black eyes refused her wish. They mesmerized, entranced, and stung her heart all at the same time.

He leaned closer, his eyes burning hotter and said in a voice that she heard echo within her mind, "One name is cloaked in the breath of God, and this name is mother. Your daughter is frightened for you."

The woman's eyes widened. Her heart pounded. "How do you know my daughter? Who are you? Get away from me!"

His voice left his lips so softly, but the truth of his words echoed like trumpets in her mind. "She wears a rose-colored shawl that is too small and is tied with a tattered ribbon."

A weight like a rock dropped onto her chest, stealing her breath. "Who are you?" she croaked.

Again, he spoke, his voice soft, like a dream, only it wasn't a dream — it was a nightmare. "She is scared, but she is also tired. Mostly, she is tired of being afraid. I fear she is working up the courage to leave behind the safety of your home to find you."

Alec faltered. What he saw next cut straight to his heart. He swallowed the knot in his throat and once more locked eyes with the terrified woman. "I fear she will take to the streets..." The pain cut deeper, stealing his breath. He dropped her hand and grabbed her shoulders. "And meet her death."

The woman's face crumpled. She sobbed into her hand.

"Go to her," Alec urged, releasing her. "Go to your daughter. This world is filled with wolves. It is you who must teach her to survive." He looked the woman hard in the eye. "Protect her or she will not be long for this world."

She dropped the bottle, which shattered on a rock. Red wine pooled around the broken shards like blood. Horror carved harsh lines in her face as she stared up at Alec for a moment longer. Then she turned and ran.

Alec leaned against the stone wall, catching his breath, trying to free his body from the grip of pain prompted by his vision. But before he could expel the images and emotions, he was struck by fresh, raw anger. He looked down the road just as a man rushed another man, driving him into a banking of snow. The dark figures groaned and snarled as they pummeled each other with fists and gnashed their teeth like animals. Straightening, Alec stormed off in the opposite direction. He needed to escape the voices, the violence and suffering.

He headed down a familiar road and stopped outside the Anchor Tavern. Peering into the window, he saw many faces that matched the whirl of emotions passing through the glass and into his heart. He started to back away, changing his mind. He needed a quiet place, a place of isolation, but then the door swung open.

"I thought I saw ye out here," came a quiet voice.

Alec turned back around to see a woman standing in the doorway. He at once suppressed the mass of feeling within him, strengthening his defenses. In truth, he was relieved to see Moira, but he had no wish to enter her heart or mind.

"Come on in, Alec. Ye look like ye've been through hell and back," she whispered.

To the rest of London, Moira was called Mary, an English tavern owner. But in truth, she hailed from the Highlands. The abbot had installed Moira in the Anchor, which he secretly owned, to provide a safe house for Scotland's agents working in London.

Alec followed Moira into the tavern, passing two barmaids along the way.

"I hate the sight of him," he heard one hiss. "His manner offends me."

"He could be as mean as second skimmings, and I wouldn't care. He's gorgeous," the other maid said in reply.

Alec took a seat in the corner beside Moira, fighting to ignore the onslaught of feelings inside and outside his own body.

"Have you found the bridge you've been searching for?" Moira asked, masking her Scottish brogue.

"No," he said, not looking up into her unguarded eyes. "I'm still looking." He had always respected Moira. With her frank tongue and flaming red hair, she reminded him of his elder sister, Rose.

"It is unlike you to be so ... transfixed on something. I've never known you to ... well ... to care enough about anything."

The familiar criticisms rolled off Alec's back. The walls he built to block out the world made people believe him careless and cruel. But in truth, fire burned within him, and he cared about the lost souls around him far more than anyone knew.

"What is so special about this bridge?"

Alec was careful to keep his voice even. "My reasons are my own. It stretches over a ditch and is guarded by two stone lions, and..." his voice trailed off as one of the barmaids sauntered up to the table.

"I know what bridge you mean."

Alec looked up at her. Straightaway, he knew she was telling the truth. "Where is it, Elisa?"

Elisa shrugged. "That'll cost you." The moment the words slipped from her lips, she wished she could pluck them out of the air and swallow them back down her throat. The man's hard black eyes locked with hers, holding her gaze captive. It was like he was inside her, and she knew he would not leave until she told him what he needed to know. She tried to resist, but her heart started to pound. An icy shiver shot up her spine.

"It's near Grove Garden," she blurted.

"I've been there already."

His voice was toneless, empty, but she could feel his urgency drawing the words from her lips. "You have to go past the docks," she cried. Then she turned and hastened away.

Alec reached into his satchel and withdrew two coins, which he tossed on the table. "Give one to the girl," he told Moira.

She just looked up at him, shaking her head. "It's that important?"

"It is," he whispered, avoiding her gaze. But then he leaned in, straining to guard his mind against the influx of Moira's memories, as he pressed a kiss to her cheek. "Be careful," he said. Then he turned and left the tavern.

Only the most desperate souls wandered the streets at night. Heedless of dangers, some even welcomed the greedy assault of a thief, hoping to end their suffering with a quick death. Guarding his heart and mind against the bleak night, Alec kept his head down. Finally, Grove Garden came into view. He hastened beyond the docks just as Elisa had advised. Then he saw it. Wrought iron rails curled with even greater detail than in his dream, and posted on each side of the rails was a stone lion. He approached the bridge, scanning his surroundings. It did, indeed, pass over a large ditch, but the lions' faces appeared different than in his vision. They were fearsome as if they guarded the bridge for themselves rather than being the silent sentries he had imagined. He hurried across the bridge and stood in the place the woman in his vision had stood. He gripped the railing and closed his eyes, welcoming a vision, anything to help him unravel the mystery.

But the only thing that reared its head was the rising sun and a burgeoning crowd of people filing into the streets to begin their day. Chaos from the growing number of passersby fought to enter his mind. He tried to shield himself from the din, but it was all too much. The time had come for him to return to his quiet chamber in the king's palace.

Chapter Four

"I'm going to change the mustard plaster again," Joanie said, laying her hand on Diana's brow.

Diana's lips curved into the slightest smile. "Thank you for all you do," she whispered.

Joanie swallowed back her tears, for she knew she had reached the limits of her knowledge. Diana's coughing attacks were coming more frequently and lasting longer. Not only had she been kept out all night by the master, but she had also been forced to endure his physical demands. The sun had fully cleared the horizon by the time she had opened the door to their room. Joanie nearly had to carry Diana to the bed. Now, as she lay beneath the covers, she shivered, and a raspy sound followed her every breath.

Diana seized Joanie's hand the instant before another coughing fit laid claim to her fragile body. Joanie could hear the illness's origins deep within her lungs. Diana gagged, and Joanie reached for the basin to catch what emerged from Diana's lungs. Quickly, Joanie whisked the basin away to the window before Diana could glimpse the blood mixed in with the yellow matter. Joanie squeezed her own eyes shut against the sight as she tilted the basin, releasing the hopelessness of Diana's condition to the cobblestones below.

Despair made Joanie's mind race. What should she do? She considered her basket of remedies and started to reach once more for the mustard powder. But then she heard her grandmother's voice in her head...

There comes a time, Joanie, when a healer must surrender hope, when all that is left to do is to soothe and comfort.

Joanie closed her eyes. She could picture her grandmother darting around her small hut, pinching powders from clay pots and mixing juices and oils to make potions and ointments with the power to take away the hurt.

She released a long breath that did nothing to ease the dread that gripped the pit of her stomach. Then she opened her eyes and looked at Diana whose breaths came in shallow rasps. Joanie knew the time had finally come when she needed to focus not on trying to heal Diana, but to bring her as much comfort as she could. She turned to her basket and sifted through the pouches and pots. Cursing under her breath, she realized she was out of Coltsfoot. Simon, whose arrival she expected at any moment, would, no doubt, fetch some from the kitchens for her. In the meantime, she set a soothing tisane to boil. Then she rubbed some lavender oil just under Diana's nose to help loosen her tense body.

"Joanie, you needn't fret so over me," Diana said, her voice barely above a whisper. "This will pass. It always does."

Joanie swallowed her doubt and smiled, taking Diana's hand. "Of course it will," she said, allowing herself to hope.

Diana smiled weakly. "Sing me one of your grandmother's songs. Your voice alone could heal me." Then her eyes opened a little wider. "No, wait. Tell me about how she used to kiss you goodnight."

Joanie smiled sadly, brushing a wayward lock of flaxen hair from Diana's eye. While Joanie had at least experienced true love and affection from her grandmother, Diana had been abandoned at birth and had no memory of her family. Her first six years were spent in an impoverished convent where she slept in a room with dozens of other children. The sisters would bring them gruel in the morning, then again in the evening, which they would eat on their flea-ridden pallets. In all the years she spent there, she never once left that room, which she said froze in winter and broiled in summer. Then, one day, the sisters came to them crying. They said the convent had no more money, and they had been unable to find another willing to take on more hungry bellies. With swollen, tearful eyes, the sisters released Diana and the other children out onto the streets to fend for themselves.

She lived for months on the streets, hiding and scavenging. Then one day, she was spotted by a woman with garish makeup and unbound hair. She called herself Honey Faintree. Honey took Diana home to her brothel, gave Diana her name, and put her to work as a maid serving the women in Honey's employ. Diana was not treated harshly but neither was she shown any kindness. Honey told her kindness was a lie, and that Diana had to be hard if she were going to stay warm and fed, warm and fed being the highest of aspirations.

Honey protected Diana from her clients' amorous advances but not their fists or swift kicks if she failed at a task. Then on her fifteenth birthday, Honey declared Diana a woman grown and made her take her place among the other prostitutes. Diana's beauty was such that not a whole year passed before a man came forward with coin enough to buy her outright. Since then, Diana had known three masters, including Geoffrey.

Joanie again smoothed Diana's hair away from her eyes. It was no wonder after being abandoned, then bought and sold time and again that Diana loved to listen to stories about Joanie's grandmother who had also been the one light in Joanie's otherwise dark world.

Joanie's own mother had died long before Joanie could remember. And her father had been a cruel man. Most evenings, he would sink into his cups and let loose his fists, beating Joanie nearly every day of her life. Her grandmother had tried to interfere but in doing so would only incur the abuse of her cruel son-in-law for herself.

When Joanie grew in size and strength, she pleaded with her grandmother to step down, arguing she was strong and could withstand the might of her father's fist. Truthfully, Joanie was physically no match for her father, but her body always healed quicker than most. More than that, she could remove herself from the pain and disappear into a world all her own, never giving her father the satisfaction of hearing her plea for mercy or cry out in pain. The first and last time he ever saw her cry was when he told her that her grandmother had died. It was not long after that her father sold her to a merchant passing through town. She had hoped her new owner would show her mercy, but he was as quick to temper as her father. She passed through two other hands, all cruel and biting, before she ended up being sold to a black hearted innkeeper in London who made her work from sunup until well after nightfall. It was there that she first met Diana.

Geoffrey Mercer's household had come to stay at the inn, filling several rooms. Late one morning, Joanie had entered the merchant's room to change the linens, believing it to be empty. But when she spotted Diana lying on the bed, she gasped and quickly backed away, uttering an apology for the intrusion. Diana, however, stopped her with a smile and beckoned Joanie to her bedside. Joanie remembered feeling spellbound by the sight of Diana. She had never seen a woman so beautiful, but more than that, Diana's eyes shone with kindness, something she had not glimpsed since before her grandmother's passing.

"What is your name?" Diana had asked.

"Joanie," she whispered.

"Joanie," she said as if she were tasting it. "I like your name. It is strong."

Joanie did not know how to answer or if she were even allowed, so she held her tongue, waiting for Diana to give her instruction. But then Diana's eyes shut. "Forgive me, Joanie, my head pains me."

Without thinking, Joanie stepped closer and placed a hand on Diana's head and focused the direction of her spirit to the places that hurt just as her grandmother had shown her. After a few moments, Diana's lips curved upward, and she opened her eyes. "The pain is gone," she said in awe. "How did you do that?"

Joanie backed away, her shoulders lifting protectively around her ears. "My grandmother was a healer," she said quietly.

Diana smiled at her. "You will have to tell me about her sometime. For now, however, I am late. Would you mind helping me dress?"

Joanie had already lingered too long. Her chores were piling up. Still, risking the innkeeper's wrath, she stayed and helped Diana.

When she was dressed and ready to quit the room, Diana gave Joanie a silver coin. "You are almost enough to make me believe in angels," Diana said, smiling. Then her smiled faltered. "Almost."

Joanie, who would sooner believe in faeries and wood nymphs than she would angels, looked up at Diana's striking green eyes and halo of golden hair, and for a moment, despite the hardships she routinely faced, she almost believed in angels too ... almost.

"I must go," Diana said. Then she squeezed Joanie's hand and dashed from the room.

That night, Joanie crawled onto her thin pallet in the corner of the basement, gripping her coin in her hand. She held it close like a friend and was drifting to sleep when loud footfalls thundered down the stairs. Joanie's heart pounded as she hid her coin beneath her pallet just before the innkeeper appeared, his pitted, red face illuminated by the lamp he held above his head.

He kicked her in the gut. "Get up," he snarled down at her, spittle flecking his lips. "You're leaving."

Unable to breathe, Joanie scurried back against the wall, but he snarled and lunged for her. She darted away, leaving behind her threadbare cloak and the coin and tore up the stairs while she gasped for air.

"Get from my sight," the innkeeper shouted, racing up the stairs behind her.

She trained her eyes on the front door, fear and confusion fighting for domination in her mind. She did not know what she had done.

She grabbed the door handle the instant before the innkeeper kicked her from behind, and she tumbled out onto the streets. Pain shot through her as she looked up and met Diana's kind eyes.

Hope suddenly filled Joanie's heart, sweeping the pain away. Mayhap angels were, indeed, real.

Brows drawn with concern, Diana bent and offered Joanie her hand.

"Did I tell you to help it stand," a harsh voice snapped.

Joanie's eyes darted away from Diana's, and she looked up and met another pair of cold, hard eyes. She knew in that moment that she was looking at her new master. And when Diana stood straight and obediently withdrew her offered hand, she also knew he was Diana's master.

So much for angels.

Later that same night, Joanie learned that having felt her healing touch, Diana had persuaded Geoffrey to buy Joanie as her maid. And they had been together ever since.

"Tell me about how your grandmother kissed you goodnight," Diana whispered again, bringing Joanie's thoughts back to the present.

Joanie smiled. "She would first kiss my forehead. Then she..."

Diana's cough returned. The pain shattered her beautiful features.

Joanie stood up. "I will wait no longer. Simon must be detained. I am going to the kitchens myself."

Diana's eyes widened in alarm. "Nay, Joanie. If Geoffrey catches you, he'll kill you."

"Do not worry, Diana. No one will see me. He is likely still sleeping off the drink from last night."

Diana reached out and weakly gripped Joanie's arm. "Please, don't do this."

Joanie pressed a kiss to Diana's forehead, then one on each cheek just as her grandmother used to do. "Rest, my dearest, and I will return before you wake."

Chapter Five

Joanie hunched over a little, keeping her shoulders up around her ears as she hastened through the castle corridors. She needed to find the servant's entrance to the kitchens, but upon arriving at the king's palace more than six months before, she had not once stepped foot from Diana's room. She knew not the hour but having yet to pass anyone other than a few of the upstairs maids in the hallway, she hoped it was still morning.

One of the maids she passed, who stood on a ladder, removing candle stubs from a candelabra, flashed her a quizzical look. But a moment later, she turned her attention back to scrapping at the remains of dried wax, which ran down the dangling silver in thin, meandering rivulets. To Joanie's relief, although not to her surprise, the maid had clearly dismissed her from her thoughts. Joanie knew that in the forefront of the maid's mind was the task she had been given and what would happen if she took too long to accomplish it. If other servants she might encounter were as equally occupied, they, too, would likely dismiss her just as quickly, which bolstered Joanie's courage. She now had reason to hope that word of her journey through the keep would not reach her master's ears.

A cold chill shot up her spine at the mere thought of him finding out she had left Diana's room. She dared not even imagine the measure of his fury. He would beat her — this much she knew for certain, but would he stop? She doubted he would stop until she was dead. Doubtless, her actions put her life in jeopardy, but for Diana, she would traverse the very fires of hell. Diana was more than her mistress. She was her dearest friend, her sister. Joanie stopped short suddenly unable to breathe, feeling as if something had grabbed her heart and squeezed until it could beat no more.

"Diana is dying," she whispered out loud.

Tears stung her eyes as she choked down a sob struggling to leave her throat. Shaking her head, she swallowed her sorrow. Diana was not dead yet. And Joanie was going to bring her every relief she could.

She turned the corner and stopped short again. A man, as straight and tall as a tower, strode down the corridor from the opposite direction. His fine tunic of rich, red velvet shimmered in the candlelight. Joanie looked away before her gaze reached his face. Her shoulders framed her ears, and she turned into the wall as she walked, trying to make herself as small and insignificant as she could. When the man walked by without uttering a word, she expelled a quiet breath. Still, encountering one of the nobles had rattled her to her core. She fisted her hands to stop them from shaking. Then her heart nigh burst with relief.

Up ahead, a young man carrying a tray of dirty mugs and bowls passed through a door. Rushing behind him came a serving maid, also bearing a tray of stacked wooden bowls. Joanie surged forward, forgetting her diminished posture in her excitement. At last, she had found the servants entrance to the kitchens. Cautious again, she slowed her pace and curved her spine to reduce her height. She paused in the doorway entrance, her eyes darting left, then right. Long stone corridors stretched on either side of her, empty but for dancing shadows made by flickering candlelight. Looking straight ahead, she peered down narrow stone steps. Din from the kitchens reached her ears. Several different voices shouted orders, followed by the scurry of rushing feet. With a deep breath, she descended.

The narrow passage opened to a wide, bustling room. Several large cuts of meat were roasting in preparation for dinner. Two massive iron cauldrons bubbled with stew. She hurried past a young boy dumping a bucket of water into a deep, stone sink. Weaving through rows of tables, lined with servants chopping vegetables and plucking fowl, she kept her head low, but her eyes darted around the room. Then she saw it, the herb cupboard.

On the far side of the room, a tall woman with a slim build had flung wide two slatted doors, revealing shelves of pots in varying sizes. The kitchen maid ran her finger along the top shelf, gently grazing each vessel until she reached a round, red-clay pot. Taking it down, she set it on the table behind her and scooped a large handful of what Joanie recognized as rosemary into a bowl. Then she returned the pot and shut the cupboard doors before hastening over to one of the large, steaming cauldrons.

Wanting to be certain the maid did not plan on returning to the cupboard, Joanie held her breath and watched while she deftly stirred the rosemary into the stew. When she set down her spoon and joined another table where several servants stood kneading bread, Joanie shifted her gaze back to the cupboard. She counted to three in her head to find her courage, then set off across the busy room, dodging servants with teeming trays.

Her heart pounded and her hands shook as she eased open the cupboard doors, fully expecting at any moment for someone to bark at her from behind ... *What do you think you're doing? You don't belong here!*

Each pot had a label fixed on with wax, but she could not read. Her heart threatened to break free from her chest, it pounded so hard. Still, she pushed on, grabbing one of the many pots and looked inside, returning it to the shelf a moment later. Eleven pots later, she suppressed a desperate squeal of triumph that came unbidden to her lips and scooped two handfuls of Coltsfoot, filling the pouch she had brought in her satchel before she returned the pot and closed the doors. Turning on her heel, she dropped her head low and took another deep breath before she set out across the bustling kitchen.

The doorway loomed before her. She skirted around another boy with a bucket of water and took her first step up the stairs when a voice she knew boomed throughout the kitchen. Silence followed in its wake as everyone froze, including Joanie.

"My master did not enjoy his meal. Nothing was salted properly," the man growled.

Joanie's heart sank. It was Simon. She did not mean to glance his way. In fact, she was certain she had told her feet to run, but instead they locked eyes. His nostrils flared and his face grew red as he narrowed his eyes on her and crossed the room. Joanie stood her ground, knowing it was pointless to run. She fought to keep her fear at bay as she watched his approach. After all, Simon was not a cruel man. He had always shown Diana true compassion and Joanie gentle indifference, which was the next closest thing to kindness she had ever experienced. When he reached her side, he grabbed her arm and pulled her halfway up the stairs.

"Speak quickly. And by all the saints, please have a good reason for being here."

"Diana—" she began quietly.

He grabbed her shoulders. "What about Diana?" he hissed.

"She ... she is worse than ever. She suffers. I needed Coltsfoot to ease her pain, but my stores were out."

Simon raked his hand through his thinning hair. "Were you able to the find it?"

She nodded, her heart still racing.

"The master has already finished eating. He could be heading back to the wing as we speak. If you value your life at all, you will race back to the room."

Eyes wide with fear, Joanie nodded her head. Then she turned and sprinted up the stairs. Blindly, she raced down the corridor, fear tightening her chest. She turned the wrong way and found a wing with a garderobe but no further stairs. A sob escaped her lips when she realized her mistake. Turning on her heel, she charged back the way she'd come. Tears blurred the path. Panting, she turned the corner and raced down a long corridor with a tapestry that looked familiar. Her master occupied the rooms of the southern wing, and she felt in her heart she was almost there. But just then a hand grabbed her arm. It didn't pinch or hurt, but it brought her race to a halt.

She gasped. Craning her neck back, she met the coldest, blackest eyes she had ever seen. Long, ebony hair hung past his shoulders, and his face was smooth, stark white and expressionless. She cried out, turning her eyes away while she frantically struggled to yank her arm free.

ALEC COULD NOT BELIEVE his eyes, although he guarded his surprise behind his usual façade of indifference. Still, it was she, the lass from his vision. He held her in his grasp. Her wide eyes filled her small, pale face like bright amber moons. Fear raged through her like wildfire, hotter even than the stone suddenly scorching his skin. It was her fear, in fact, that had drawn him to her. He had felt it in the hallway before he had even glimpsed her from a distance. He followed, not suspecting she was his mystery lass, but to ensure the girl did not face real danger. It was not until the very moment he looked into her familiar eyes and the stone around his neck nigh erupted into flame that he realized who she was.

"'Tis ye," he said aloud.

The very fear that had led him to her, only grew the longer he held her arm. Her eyes widened further, and her heartbeat pounded harder until he thought his head might split.

"I will not hurt ye," he whispered.

"Let go of me," she cried. Her body began to tremble. Panic threatened to claim her, which he knew would put all reason out of reach. He had no choice but to let her go.

The moment he released her hand, she darted away toward the southern wing.

He stared after her, his mind still reeling with the might of her fear and the reality that the lass from his vision was, at that very moment, in the king's palace. When he had touched her, he saw the flash of an old woman's face with kind, faded blue eyes, but that was all. Usually, he experienced an assault of feelings and images when he touched someone. Now, she was gone from sight. Still, he could feel her fear. Who was she? Why did the stone respond to her presence? She was an English servant — how could she be important to the cause? And why was her soul seeking his?

He pressed his hand over the shard, feeling the heat through his tunic. He needed answers. For a moment, he considered questioning some of the servants, but then he thought better of it. Most of the palaces' servants feared him. What's more, he could not trust their tongues not to wag. He stretched his neck to the right, then the left, realizing there was only one way to find the answers he sought. He would have to attend supper that night in the great hall.

Chapter Six

Joanie threw the door open, her heart pounding, but she quietly shut it to not alarm Diana. She rested her back against the door and closed her eyes, overcome with relief that she had not been caught — at least by the master. When she gained control of her breathing, she crossed the room to where Diana lay. She sat down beside her on the bed and gently rested her hand on Diana's forehead. She felt a little warm, but at least she was resting soundly. Joanie took the pouch out of her satchel and crumbled some of the dried green leaves into the bubbling kettle, which simmered over the fire. Waiting for the leaves to steep, her mind drifted back to the strange man in the hallway. He had been so tall, leanly built, and achingly beautiful, but his eyes had been so bleak. She had felt as if she stared into a great shadowy abyss where no light could ever shine. And when he touched her, she felt currents of heat flow from his body into hers as if he had tried to invade her very soul. What sort of man had such power?

Diana groaned in her sleep, pulling Joanie to the present. She pushed the stranger from her thoughts. He did not matter. Joanie had no intention of leaving Diana's room again; thus, she would never again see his black eyes or feel his blazing touch.

After a few hours, a knock sounded at the door, and a servant from the kitchen came in. She did not look at Joanie or Diana — they never did. She simply walked in, set the tray down, then left. Joanie glanced at the food. As always, it was a tray for one. Joanie looked over at Diana, still sleeping. So, she moved the tray over to the hearth to keep the broth and meat warm. At different points, Diana awoke and coughed up more phlegm and much to Joanie's alarm even more blood. Then she would fall back down onto her pillow and immediately succumb to sleep.

Long after the sun reached its highest point in the sky, Diana awoke.

"Joanie," she rasped.

Joanie pressed her hand to Diana's forehead. "I'm here," she said.

"I'm glad," Diana breathed.

"Do you think you could sit up a little?"

Diana nodded and started to lift her head, but then she winced. "I ache everywhere."

"Keep still then, but you must drink some broth." Joanie supported Diana's head with one hand and tipped the bowl to her lips.

After swallowing barely a thimble's worth, Diana signaled she'd had enough. "Thank you," she whispered.

Joanie gently set her head back down on the pillow and returned the bowl to the hearth.

"What have you had to eat?" Diana asked, her voice raw.

"Don't worry about me," Joanie said.

"It is not worry, Joanie. It is love. You are my family, my sister."

Tears welled in Joanie's eyes. "Just rest, Diana, you need your strength."

A slight smile curved Diana's lips. "I think I will." She closed her eyes, a look of peace shaping her features only to be marred by panic an instant later. "Saints above, what is the hour?"

"It is nones?"

"Why did you not say?" Diana cried, straining to sit up.

Joanie rushed to her bedside. "You cannot get up."

"But Joanie, I must."

Joanie shook her head, gently pressing her hands into Diana's shoulders to keep her still.

"I need to get ready. I am singing tonight." Diana's eyes darted around the room wildly.

"Diana, look at me," Joanie said softly.

Diana held Joanie's gaze for several moments, and then tears flooded her eyes. "I can't sing, can I?" she whispered.

Joanie pressed her lips together to contain her own tears, and shook her head in reply, not trusting herself to speak.

"What am I going to do?" Diana cried, covering her face with her hands.

Just then a knock sounded at the door. Joanie looked up just as Simon entered and hastened to Diana's bedside. "How are you?" he asked.

Joanie backed away to give them space. Mayhap, Simon would know what to do. She watched as he sat down and covered Diana's hand with his. Stepping farther away, she retreated to where she would not hear their whispered words.

"No," Diana snapped, drawing Joanie's gaze. She stood and returned to the bed, crossing her arms over her chest, ready to do battle with Simon if need be.

"There is no other way," Simon said, his voice strained with frustration.

Diana looked away. "My answer is final."

Simon withdrew his hand and stiffened in his seat. "It isn't really up to you." Then he turned and locked eyes with Joanie.

"You will be singing tonight," he said simply.

Joanie felt her limbs tremble. Her arms fell slack at her sides.

"Don't listen to him, Joanie. He..." Diana said, straining to raise her voice. Her last words were lost to her cough.

Joanie reached for Diana's shoulders. "Help me lift her head," she said to Simon.

When her cough subsided, Diana lay in a weakened state as if lost in a thick fog.

Simon grabbed Joanie's arm. "You will sing in her stead," he said, his voice harsh.

Joanie winced. "I cannot ... I am not like her. I'm not beautiful. I'm not—"

"Your voice is," Simon interrupted. "I've heard you sing to her. And though you are not beautiful in the same way, you are unique. There is a boldness to your features, and your voice ... I've never heard anything like it before." He grabbed her hands, his voice now pleading. "She can't do it. She will collapse on stage and be ruined."

"Don't listen to him," Diana croaked.

Joanie yanked her hands free from Simon's grasp and hastened to Diana's side.

"What Simon will not tell you is that he is only seeks to spread out Geoffrey's fury among us all, so that I alone do not bear the brunt of it. But I am the one who is unable to fill my role. I alone should be punished."

Now Joanie understood Simon's intent. She certainly would invite the master's anger were she to take Diana's place.

In fact, her offense would be so great, and Simon's, too, for allowing her to sing, that Diana's absence may be overlooked entirely. She bent and pressed a kiss to Diana's cheek. Then she turned to Simon and said without hesitation, "I'll do it. I will sing."

Chapter Seven

Simon's eyes softened. He stepped toward her and cupped her cheek in his hand. "Though you may be small, you are in possession of great heart. Thank you," he whispered.

"Do not do this, Joanie," Diana said, her voice pleading. "You have already given me so much. All things must come to an end."

Joanie allowed her shoulders to drop from around her ears. She stood straight. "Now is not the end." Then she turned to Simon. "What must I do?"

"Remove your clothing. I will have servants from the kitchen bring water for a bath. They also will assist you with your...ablutions." Simon's voice trailed off as he openly scrutinized Joanie's appearance. She knew what he saw. Tattered tunic. Stiff, dirty black hair. Dull, white skin. Wide, dry lips. Instinctively, her shoulders rose to her ears once more.

"Stand up straight," he snapped. Then he turned on his heel and strode out the door.

"Joanie," Diana began.

Joanie steeled her heart against her beseeching tone. "My mind is made up. I will take the master's anger off your shoulders. I am strong. I may not look it, but I am. You know I am. I can take it, Diana; whereas ... you cannot." She felt her voice tighten as grief filled her very soul.

"Please, Joanie."

Desperation and fear forced Joanie's voice to rise. "Do not ask me to hand you over to the wolf, to surrender you to him.

You cannot ask that of me, Diana. You can't." A sob tore from her throat.

Diana opened her arms. A flood of tears burst from Joanie's eyes as she allowed Diana to enfold her in a weak embrace. "Hush, my dear sister. All right," she soothed. "We will get through this together."

Joanie lifted her head and swiped her eyes. Then she nodded.

"Go on then," Diana gently urged her. "Do as Simon bid. Take your clothes off."

Joanie took a deep breath and nodded again, not yet trusting herself to speak. Diana did not have much time. The end was nigh. But it would not be that night. And it would not be the master who took Diana from her.

She circled around the screen and shed her clothing, letting the threadbare woolen pieces drop to the floor. Her eyes scanned over her scarred, bruised body before she peeked through the cracks between the panels of the screen toward the door, waiting fearfully for it to open.

Several minutes passed, and she shivered from the chill in the air. Scooting the screen closer to the hearth, she continued her vigil, her eyes trained on the door. Several more minutes passed when suddenly she heard footfalls echoing through the corridor. Fearing it was the master, her heart started to pound, but then she expelled a slow breath as the door swung open and Simon entered, along with several men carrying steaming buckets of water, followed by two young maids. Joanie watched through the slits in the screen as they filled the tub. Steam floated off the surface.

"Come out from there," Simon said, his voice not unkind but certainly commanding. Joanie jumped at the sound. She scanned the room still teeming with servants.

"No," she hissed.

"Dismiss the men," she heard Diana say the instant before another coughing fit set in.

"Diana," Joanie said, peering with concern through the crack in the screen.

"I will take care of her," Simon said. Then he barked several commands as he slid his arm behind Diana's head and held the bowl to catch the spittle from her lips. "The men are gone. Only the two maids remain. Now, come out."

Joanie eyed the young serving girls for a moment. Then her gaze settled back on Simon. A moment later, he answered the question plaguing her mind.

"I am not leaving. This plan falls on my head too. I will make sure your appearance is right. Now, come out from behind that screen and get into the tub, or I will come around and toss you in there myself. Do you understand?"

Joanie's eyes widened. She knew Simon's threat was not idly made. Taking a deep breath, she scurried from behind the screen, her hands covering her nakedness.

"Dear God," Simon gasped.

Startled, she turned her head and met his gaze. She saw the horror in his eyes as he scanned the back of her naked body. She knew what he saw — a lifetime of fists, lashes, and worse had left their mark on her skin. Awash in shame, she hid her head between her shoulders and quickly climbed into the tub, sinking beneath the surface to hide from the world. Only her need to breathe forced her to resurface. The moment her head broke through, hands started to scrub and wash her body.

"Be gentle," she heard Simon snap.

One of the servants washed her hair with a bar of perfumed soap while the other girl scrubbed her arms, breasts, stomach, and legs with a rough soapy rag. When she was done, she dropped the rag and scooped a mix of oil and crushed nuts with which she attacked Joanie's body until her skin felt raw. She sputtered when a bucket of water poured down over her head.

"Lay your head back and upturn your face," one of the girls said.

Joanie did as she was bid and closed her eyes. She winced as the oil and nuts raked her skin. The girl pressed it into her cheeks and forehead and neck in hard circular motions. Then she cupped water in her hands and rinsed away the residue. Joanie breathed deep the heavy scent of lavender while the maid rubbed just the oil gently into her cheeks and brow, soothing away the hurt. She closed her eyes and tried to surrender to the calming scent. But then she winced when she heard Simon say, "Her eyebrows are too thick." A moment later the touch of cool metal grazed her forehead. She gripped the sides of the tub as hair after hair was plucked from her brow.

"That's better," Simon said with approval.

A moment later, a warm thick paste was being pressed onto her face. The sweet smell of porridge and honey made her stomach growl, reminding her she had not eaten a bite that day. She resisted the urge to lick off a morsel to ease her hunger pains.

"Enough," Simon said.

She could hear the impatience in his voice. Or was it nerves?

"We must allow time for her hair to dry. Get her out of the tub and continue her treatments near the hearth."

Instantly, she felt hands reach under her arms. "I can get up on my own," she snapped, and she started to stand. But then the cool air hit her nakedness. She rushed to cover herself, sinking back beneath the water. How could Diana do this, day after day, allowing hands to paw her and eyes to see her body? Joanie's face burned.

"Do you need my help?" Simon's voice held a warning. She shook her head and stood, hunched over, her hands trying to shield her body from the many eyes in the room.

"Stand up straight," Simon snapped again.

Slowly, she unraveled and stood straight with her hands at her sides. He came around to the front of her and scrutinized her. He took her hands and turned them over.

"Who knew you had such a body hiding under your clothes," Diana said weakly from the bed.

"If you can look past the battle scars," Simon said, scowling. "Still, your figure has more curve than I would have guessed, which is a relief. But the condition of your hands is appalling. We will do our best, but you will likely have to wear gloves." He tipped his thumb under her chin. "Open your eyes, Joanie."

She held her breath and dug deep to find her courage and forced her lids to open.

There was nothing salacious or mocking in Simon's gaze. He looked at her sternly. "Just because you are common does not mean you must be common. Stand up straight."

She expelled a short breath, fear and shame swirled around her in dizzying emotional waves. "I am nothing," she blurted.

"Those are your father's words," Diana said. "Do not make them your own."

Simon inspected her face. "Her skin needs no paint. Her fairness would be the envy of every woman at court. Apply lemon juice to her lips. And line her eyes to show off their size. Just a dash of rouge. And brush her hair out and let it fall freely. When it's dry, oil it. Choose a tunic with a high neckline to cover her scars, but take it in so that it is fitted to her curves. I will return in a few hours to see how you progress."

Sometime later, Joanie stood very still while one of the maids shortened Diana's sapphire blue tunic. When she was finished, she tied a belt tightly around Joanie's waist. Then she dabbed perfumed oil behind her ear and on the inside of her wrists. Meanwhile, the other maid continued what she had been doing for at least an hour — rubbing thick cream made from hog fat and lavender oil into her hands.

When Simon returned, he didn't bother knocking. He walked into the room, straight over to where she stood. He scrutinized every inch of her, straightening her belt, checking the evenness of her hemline. He lifted her chin and turned her face from side to side. Then he stepped back and brought a hand to his bearded chin as he continued his scrutiny. Just as Joanie was about to race back behind the screen, a slight smile curved Simon's lips. He grabbed Diana's hand mirror off her bedside table and held it in front of Joanie.

"Do you still believe you are nothing?" Simon asked softly.

Joanie didn't recognize the woman looking back at her. This stranger had shiny ebony waves, pinned up on one side with a sprig of dried lavender. Her brown eyes, outlined in charcoal, gleamed like amber jewels. The color of her lips had taken on a deep blush from the lemon juice and stood out in shocking contrast to her fair skin, which shone with bright vitality. Her brows were thin and perfectly arched. Her heart started to pound, and she felt her shoulders rise up as she longed to shrink away from her own reflection.

"You can hide from everyone but yourself," Simon said.

"Let me see you," Diana urged.

Joanie crossed to where her friend lay. Diana's skin looked mottled, and the rings beneath her eyes had darkened.

She smiled with approval. "My beauty is fashionable, perfectly predictable. Yours, on the other hand, is unique, powerful."

Joanie's stomach twisted. She did not wish to be beautiful. She wanted to be forgettable.

"It is time," Simon said, behind them. Her heart started to pound, but she saw fear invade Diana's peace. Fighting back her own terror, Joanie smiled gently at her mistress. "I can do this," Joanie said with forced confidence. "Simon's plan is a good one. You'll see."

Chapter Eight

Joanie walked down the long corridor of the southern wing on Simon's arm. Candlelight flickered as they passed. She strained to focus on Simon's words over the din of her own beating heart.

"Remember to stand up straight. Never rush your movements. Walk slowly, seductively. Charm every man and woman with just the shadow of a smile or the tilt of your head."

Her stomach twisted. "I have not left that room in months. For years, the only souls I've spoken to are you and Diana, and you ask me to be charming."

He grabbed her arm and stopped her, his gaze desperate. "The only hope we have of saving Diana is for you to strike wonder in everyone's heart." His grip tightened. "I've heard you sing. You don't know this, but I have stood outside the door and listened to you with bated breath." He shook his head. "There is something indescribable about your voice. It cries and rejoices all at the same time. You have it in you to steal their breath, and if you do, the master will be praised by all. He will be a champion." Simon's grip tightened still. "But if you falter, if you allow fear to be your guide, then the master will be made a fool. God save us all from that."

For a moment, Joanie sank beneath the pressure of Simon's words, but then she realized he too risked it all for Diana. "You love her, don't you?"

Simon closed his eyes and released her arm, gently taking her hand instead. "My every thought, my every breath and prayer are for her."

Tears stung Joanie's eyes, but she took a deep breath and squeezed Simon's hand before she stepped from his side and moved just behind the large screen that separated her from the high dais and beyond that, the great hall. She gripped her tunic, her mind racing about what could possibly await her on the other side. Still, no matter what she saw, she had to rise above her fear. She imagined for a moment that she was someone else. Someone who was not afraid. Someone who had been adored her whole life. Someone who knew what it meant to be loved and admired. Her grandmother's songs came to her then, filling her with images of the distant Highlands she had only seen in her dreams. She lengthened her spine and lifted her shoulders back and away from her ears.

"For Diana," she whispered. "For my grandmother." She almost took her first step, but then she paused. "For me."

With a deep breath, she stepped from behind the screen onto the high dais, which had been used as a stage since the king had moved to York and the days of revelry had begun. She opened her lips and let the first note ring out, strong and true. Pouring her heart and soul into each note, she sang of mountains high and fields of golden wheat bending in the wind. She didn't stop when one song ended, but straightaway moved to the next, slowly moving across the dais and onto the floor where full trencher tables stretched out before her. Her hips swayed to her own music of lovers who grew old together and those who died young, of fierce battles, and a mother holding her baby for the first time. Images she created in her mind hovered above the heads of the audience, trapping her gaze. In that moment, she stood alone, singing for herself.

ALEC SAT AT ONE OF the trencher tables, trying his best to ignore the revelers. The keeper's special regard for him had warranted other men's caution and disdain, which suited Alec just fine. Now, they smiled at him, wanting to flatter someone so highly prized by John, but their smiles were naught but messages of thinly veiled hostility. For their efforts, Alec simply inclined his head, not encouragement enough for anyone to approach him but also enough to not offend, ensuring he was left alone. He looked forward to the day when he could leave the king's palace for good, which would hopefully be soon. As far as the abbot was concerned, Alec's work was already done. He had passed on his report about the monks who had partaken in the keeper's unholy gatherings. More than that, he had led many of Scotland's secret rebels in a heist, stealing the king's treasure from the abbey's Chapter House. The blame of the robbery had fallen on the shoulders of a man named Richard Ash, a greedy, hateful merchant who used to frequent the keeper's galas in the palace.

It had been Richard's idea to rob the Chapter House and steal the king's treasure. He had confided his plan to Alec. But he also spoke of the wretched things he would do once the fortune was his — the enslavement of prostitutes, the ruination of whole families he blamed for his own failures — treachery Alec could never allow.

In the end, Alec organized Scotland's agents and together, they pulled off the heist themselves. Now the royal wealth was being put to good use, feeding those in need and rebuilding Scotland's army. Meanwhile the agents had put Richard on a merchant vessel heading to Venice, ensuring it would be months before he returned to England. Because the treasure and Richard disappeared at the same time, naturally the keeper assumed Richard was the thief.

Alec noticed the keeper enter from the courtyard. John sat at the head of the trencher table closest to the high dais. Alec watched as different merchants and nobles rotated in and out of the seat next to him, everyone having their turn with his ear. As if sensing his watchful eye, the keeper shifted in his seat and locked eyes with Alec, who raised his cup in greeting. But Alec did not get up and go to the keeper. Instead, the keeper stood for him.

"There is still no sign of Richard Ash?" the keeper asked under his breath when he claimed the seat next to Alec. Alec kept his senses keen, reading the keeper's true desires over what he was actually saying.

"I've heard nothing yet, but if he turns up in London, I will be one of the first to know," Alec lied, confident it would be many months before anyone spotted Richard Ash.

The keeper shook his head. Alec could sense his anxiety. "I want him found," he hissed. "When the king's men arrive, the safety of my neck will only be assured if I have another neck to give them."

Alec leaned closer. "You've already sent a message to the king about the robbery." This wasn't a question. Alec knew he had.

The keeper shrugged, feigning indifference, but Alec could feel his pounding heart. "I thought it better if I reveal what has happened, then for it to be discovered by someone else on my watch." The keeper started to get up. "You will tell me if you hear anything?"

Alec nodded. "You know I will," he lied.

As soon as he aided the lass from his vision, Alec would leave the palace and England altogether, and he could only hope to never return. He considered asking the keeper about who occupied the southern wing, but he decided to question someone who would be less curious about why he was asking.

Once more, his mind returned to the lass. He had felt her pain so deeply. It cut a fiery path straight to his heart, bypassing all the shields he had spent years erecting. But why this girl? Why her fear, and why now? Everyone he encountered was afraid of something. He leaned back and looked around. Across from him sat a man nearing his fiftieth year. His shoulders stooped over his tankard as he eyed the young serving girls. He feared death. Farther down the table was an older prostitute whose smile hid her fear for the health of her youngest daughter who, at that moment, was lost to fever. She had wanted nothing more than to remain by her side, but she needed coin to pay for the doctor and medicine. A young man who raised his cup, making toast after toast, feared being found less than his older brothers. Illness, betrayal, failure, the wrath of God — everyone was afraid of something.

"Where have you been these last weeks, Randolph?"

Alec looked up at Sir Hugh Godfrey. There was no man vainer and shallower than Sir Hugh, which was why Alec did not offend him like he did the others. In fact, he seemed to admire Alec's indifference, thinking it evidence of his discerning taste. Sir Hugh smoothly sat down. Alec abhorred his type most of all. He was like a snake, smooth, charming, seemingly polite and chivalric, but every word from his lips was a lie.

"I've not felt well," Alec said.

Sir Hugh's brows drew together. "I'm glad you're on the mend."

Lie.

"Thank you," Alex said, his voice flat. But then he realized Sir Hugh was the perfect man to question about the Southern wing. He thought of only himself. His discretion was guaranteed, but only because he possessed the depth of a puddle.

Alec kept his eyes trained forward as if he watched the serving maids briskly moving about the room. "Who occupies the last rooms on the southern wing?"

Sir Hugh jerked his head toward a large man at the keeper's table. "Geoffrey Mercer and his leman, Diana. His manservant also has one of the rooms and so on."

"Diana," Alec said her name aloud. He remembered seeing her the night before. He remembered feeling her failing body. "She has a lovely voice," Alec said absently.

Sir Hugh shrugged. "I don't see what all the fuss is about."

Lie.

"She isn't that beautiful," he continued.

Lie.

A vision of Sir Hugh soliciting Diana in the great hall when Geoffrey was preoccupied in conversation with the keeper flashed in Alec's mind. Diana had refused him. "Yes, you are, indeed, a man of discerning taste," Alec said dryly as he stood.

Now that he had obtained the information he needed, he was ready to leave. But then he felt the shard of stone against his chest begin to heat. He scanned the room for the serving girl and spied a maid wiping a spill on one of the trencher tables in the back. Long, tangled black hair made him take a closer look. He crossed the room and stood behind her.

"Excuse me," he said not wanting to intrude upon her mind by touching her.

The girl turned.

He bowed his head. "I thought you were someone else."

With wide eyes, the girl quickly bobbed up and down in the fastest curtsy Alec had ever seen. Then she backed away from him and turned on her heel and made a dash for the kitchen. Alec was not surprised, however. Like the rest of the world, she believed him cruel and cold.

He turned away and started toward the wide doors that led out into the courtyard, but then he froze. He felt the emotion of her song before the first fragile note traveled through the air to his ears. As the sound penetrated his mind, the stone scorched his chest. His nostrils flared against the burning heat, but when he turned and saw the elegant figure standing on the high dais, the pain was forgotten. Could the polished and painted girl be the same girl he had encountered in the hallway? The figure on stage was clad in deep blue finery. She moved slowly across the floor, her eyes trained above the heads of the revelers as if she stared at a distant horizon known only to her. Her unbound dark hair curled in thick, shiny waves to her waist. Her pale skin glowed warmly in the candlelight, and her eyes were outlined in smoky color, giving her an exotic look. Her voice rasped from her throat, low and languid. Then it climbed clear and pure to the highest notes as effortlessly as if she sighed.

She stood there in plain sight, but her soul was somewhere above them all, flying through clouds of soft memories. Again, a vision flashed in Alec's mind of an older woman with warm, faded blue eyes. He could feel the love the woman had for the girl on the stage. And he could feel the security she had once known in the older woman's presence. Their bond was powerful and strong, fueling the girl's strength. What radiated from her soul was so different than the all-consuming fear he had felt from the girl in the hallway. He walked forward, joining the others who had moved to get a closer look. She slowly glided to one side of the high dais, then descended the stairs onto the main floor.

She was an angel. Her voice reached the rafters and shattered around him. Then her powerful notes suddenly shifted and crooned into a fragile caress of sound. Images so beautiful swirled around his mind of green forests and stormed-tossed seas. He knew of what she sang. He could see the rugged Highland mountains and moors of purple heather. Then, despite the demands of her own soul, she looked at the front table, and it felt as if Alec had been punched in the gut.

For a moment, he struggled to draw breath. He had opened his soul to her song, and now her fear crashed down around him. He fell back and grabbed the table behind him to catch his fall. He shook his head, trying to dispel the sudden dizziness. Her voice still reached his ears. She had not stopped her song, but he could barely hear her music above the din of her pounding heart. Her fear had returned with all the force he had felt in his dreams. It was thick and viscous, making his limbs heavy. On the outside, he knew his mask of cold indifference held, and yet on the inside he had to fight to push beyond her terror. He stood his ground and harnessed his strength, barring her from his soul. His vision cleared, and he took the sight of her in, still ensuring his own eyes revealed none of his emotions. Her gaze remained fixed on the floor. He could feel her desire to shield herself. But from what? From whom? Then another emotion cut its way into the mix. Beneath her fear fury burned, fierce and lashing — the sort that was felt in the deepest places of the heart where only truth dwells. Alec opened his eyes and looked at the source of her anger and saw the merchant, Geoffrey. But Geoffrey appeared oblivious to everything around him other than her appeal.

Alec scanned the room. Men stared in rapture. Lust dominated the room — so much so that he imagined if feelings had color, slow pulsing swaths of red would be weaving around the tables and benches, pouring from the men's bodies like beckoning fingers of desire for the girl. Each one wanting to snatch her away for himself.

Suddenly, her spirit lifted and the fear that had held him in its grip eased away. He noticed greater boldness in her step and felt her heightened confidence and unmistakable relief. Why her fear had dissipated, he could not guess. She moved among the tables, her rich voice binding the men to her as she passed. Then she approached the table where Alec stood. They locked eyes. Hers narrowed in confusion, and then an instant later, he knew she recognized him as the man in the hallway earlier that morning. She held his gaze. He did not look away. He felt her fear rebuilding like wood tossed on a fire. It sparked and grew until hot flames of it licked his insides. Her song continued, but she backed away from him like a prey retreating from a predator.

JOANIE TURNED AWAY from Geoffrey, her voice crooning notes faithfully, but inside she struggled to keep from laughing hysterically and crying with relief. Geoffrey had not recognized her. She was sure of it. Eventually, he was bound to discover the nameless singer was his servant, but at least for now she was safe from his fury. She turned away and proceeded around a cluster of tables. The men stared at her with open admiration. Never had she ever felt the warm eyes of a man on her. Never had she known what it meant to be desired. It was thrilling and terrifying all at once. One part of her wished to flee from their unwavering gazes while another part wanted to savor the honeyed warmth of being desired. She infused her song with greater passion. She was singing her favorite of her grandmother's songs about lovers forbidden to wed who fled from their families and found themselves trapped within a tempest that raged across the moors. They were swept away by the wind and landed in a place of enchantment where love conquered all. Emboldened by the heated gazes, the feel of silk against her skin, and the haunting sound of her own voice echoing off the high ceilings, she let her guard down and gave herself over to the game. She boldly looked the men in the eye but fed when she met black eyes as cold and distant as the night sky ... familiar eyes. A tremor shot up her spine as she recognized the man from earlier in the hall, and unlike Geoffrey she knew this man recognized her for who she really was. He did not look away. His face was beautiful with full lips, high cheekbones, and deep-set eyes. He wore his black hair long and straight unlike the rest of the men in the room. His tall leanly-built body exuded power in the most terrifying way. He sat perfectly still, his eyes ice cold and empty, and yet he seemed to reverberate feeling, like he was secretly shaking the room but only he and she knew it.

She started to back away. Her instinct was to flee, back to Diana, back to Geoffrey even, anyone but him and his endless, powerful gaze. She looked away, moving to the tables on the far side of the hall. With a last, lingering note that started out soaring from her lips but ended in a near whisper, she finished her song. The room erupted into cheers with an intensity that shocked her. She scurried back. Geoffrey stood with everyone else, cheering and clapping, his eyes heavy with drink and desire — he had never looked at her like that before and a warning crept up her spine. She jerked around to find the other man in the room she feared, but his seat was empty. He had gone. She bowed her head, her true self returning in a blush that burned her face with warmth. She dipped into a low curtsy and turned to mount the stairs to the high dais. She had to force her feet to walk, but her heart sprinted ahead, pounding in her chest. She rounded the screen and gasped as she met hollow, black eyes.

Chapter Nine

Alec stood just behind the screen, waiting for the lass. He felt her trepidation, before she circled around. Fear surged through her when she saw him. He grabbed her arm and pulled her close, pressing his hand across her lips just in time to smother her scream. He prepared his heart and mind for the onslaught of images and memories that would be revealed to him when he touched her ... but he saw nothing, not even the old woman whom he had glimpsed when he had grabbed her arm earlier in the hallway. Stunned, he dropped his hand. He could still feel her emotions — fear at the moment, and he could hear her pounding heart. Still, he had touched her and saw nothing, no window into her soul. But then the vision of her standing on the bridge, her wide dark eyes brimming with tears flashed in his mind, and once more he heard his name on her lips. Whether she knew it or not, her soul was reaching out to him. Why, he could not say. He had not even learned her name.

"Who are you?" he asked.

Joanie's heart raced as she considered his question. His voice was not what she had expected. It was deep but flat, as emotionless as his eyes.

"No one," she said, backing away from him and turning up the stairs. He followed behind, his long strides easily overtaking hers.

He stepped around her to stand in front of her, but to her relief he did not grab her again. He did, however, block her escape.

"What is your name?"

Joanie wanted to scream, *why do you care*? She needed to get back to the room to change out of Diana's clothing. She did not want Geoffrey to see her in the room dressed as she was. Eventually, he would know that she was the singer — but she thought being seen in Diana's finery would only fuel his ire.

"What is your name?" he repeated in the same flat voice.

She fisted her hands at her side to keep herself from lashing out with her tongue in frustration. Whoever he was he exuded danger. "I am no one of consequence."

"What is your name?"

"Margaret," she answered, giving her grandmother's name.

He stepped closer. "Do not lie to me."

Her eyes widened with surprise. "Joanie," she blurted, her heart pounding.

His expression was unreadable as were his dark eyes that, despite their emptiness, seemed to penetrate her very soul. He was effortlessly inescapable. "You are in danger," he said, his voice still void of emotion despite his warning.

Who was he? And what did he want with her? "Let me pass," she said, her heart racing harder.

He stepped closer but did not touch her. He had not raised his voice, and yet it felt as if he had surrounded her, bound her.

"Please," she whispered, choking back on a sob. "Let me pass."

"You need to calm yourself," he said, soft and low. He reached out a hand toward her, but he stopped short of touching her. Instead, he raked his hand through his long hair. He closed his eyes. "Come away with me. Whatever it is you are afraid of, I can help. I will take you away from here."

Alarms sounded in Joanie's head. Did Geoffrey send him? Was this a test to prove her loyalty?

"Joanie," he said, drawing her gaze. He was so tall, she had to crane her neck back to meet his gaze. But a chill raked up her spine, forcing her gaze to drop. It was then she noticed his hands fisted at his side, his one betrayal of the frustration she knew was building within him. She could feel it, like heat pouring off him.

"Please," she said, "if you really want to help me, then get out of my way. I must get back to the room before..." She did not know what else to say. But she could feel herself begin to panic. "Please," she cried.

He did not move. He remained in front of her, an unbreachable wall of both fire and ice. Then at last he stepped out of the way. "Go," he snapped.

She gasped. Then she lifted the hem of her tunic and shot forward down the hall as if she was fleeing from the Devil himself. She glanced back to see if he gave chase. He stood there, watching her, his long black hair glinting in the candlelight. His black eyes stood out against his snowy white skin. She tore her gaze from his and sped up, the candles streaking past in a blur of light, and she did not slow her pace until she reached Diana's door.

Chapter Ten

Joanie threw open the door, then slammed it shut behind her. Leaning against the slatted wood, she let her head fall back as she fought to catch her breath.

"Is he coming?" Diana blurted from where she sat in bed, her knuckles white from squeezing the fold of her blanket.

"No," Joanie said, breathless. "At least I don't think so." And then she realized Diana couldn't have known about the man with black eyes. She, of course, had meant the master. "I don't know when Geoffrey will come."

Diana released her death grip and smoothed the blanket over her lap. "You looked like you were running away from someone just now."

"I was," Joanie said, still trying to slow her racing heart. "But not from the master. There was another man."

Diana sat straighter. "What man? Did he hurt you? Are you alright?"

Joanie put out a calming hand. "I'm fine. He ... he frightened me, but he didn't hurt me."

"Who?"

Joanie shook her head. "I don't know his name. He was tall with very long black hair, and his eyes..." her voice trailed off as a shiver shot up her spine. "They were like the night sky before it snows — cold, empty, and teeming with power just beneath the surface."

"Ahh," Diana said, nodding knowingly. "Randolph Tweed."

Joanie hurried to Diana's bedside and sat down. "You know him?"

Diana shook her head. "I've never spoken a word to him, but I've seen him in the hall on occasion. He keeps to himself, barely speaking to anyone, his eyes as cold and unfeeling as the dead. I'm told he is favored by the keeper, but all the maids in the castle are afraid of him. One of the girls told me that he keeps to his room most of the day and only comes out at night. She says he wanders the streets. They believe he is a dark angel or even the devil himself — beautiful to look upon but wicked to his core."

Joanie's hand flew to her throat. "He bade me go away with him."

Diana's eyes widened. "He didn't?"

Joanie nodded. "He did."

Diana clasped her hand to her chest. "Keep away from him, Joanie. He has the evil eye. He'll put a curse on you or worse."

"I hope to never lay eyes upon his dark soul again," Joanie said. "I can't imagine why he approached me in the first place."

Diana laughed softly and cupped Joanie's cheek. "Whereas I am not surprised in the least. How could he resist you?" Then she sighed. "I wish I could have been there to hear you sing."

Joanie blushed and looked down at her hands at rest on blue silk. Suddenly, she drew a sharp breath. "Your tunic!" She jumped to her feet, and with trembling hands, she furtively pulled the borrowed garments over her head, which she then hung carefully in Diana's wardrobe.

She scanned the floor. "Where's my tunic," she cried to Diana, her heart once more pounding.

"Check behind the screen," Diana urged. "That is where you changed."

"Of course," Joanie said, circling around the screen where she picked up her soiled tunic and kirtle off the floor near the tub and pulled them on. Quickly plaiting her hair, she then crossed the room to the basin and washed the rouge from her cheeks and the charcoal from her eyes.

"Did I get it all?" she asked, returning to Diana's bedside.

"Yes, but it makes no difference. You are still beautiful. How did Geoffrey react when he saw you?"

"I am confident he did not know it was me."

Diana's eyes widened. "But that's wonderful. Then he never has to know." She pointed toward the hearth. "Dust ash on your face. Put oil in your hair."

Joanie shook her head. "No, Diana. I did this to protect you. Anyway, mayhap we worry for naught. Simon had hoped my performance would be celebrated, and I believe it was. The master's fury may not be as fierce as we think." She sat down and put her arms around Diana's shoulders.

"Do you really believe that?" Diana asked softly.

Joanie shrugged. "If I am wrong, I will still withstand the brunt of his anger."

"You cannot keep protecting me, Joanie."

"You cannot stop me."

Diana smiled weakly. "There is little I can stop now." A mirthless chuckle escaped her lips, soon becoming a painful cough. Joanie supported Diana's head. When her body eased, Joanie started to help Diana lay back down, but then she froze. They locked eyes. A parade of thunderous footsteps echoed down the hallway.

"The master is coming," Joanie cried.

A moment later the door flew open, and Geoffrey's massive body filled the frame. He stormed into the room, followed by his guards and Simon. He narrowed his eyes on Diana and crossed to her bedside. "Where were you?" he growled.

Joanie scurried across the bed to the opposite side, putting herself between the large, furious man and her pallid mistress. Her heart pounded like a drum in her head. Still, she met Geoffrey's gaze, lifting her chin defiantly.

"She was not well," Joanie said simply.

Geoffrey stopped in his tracks. His eyes narrowed on Joanie. And then they flashed wide, and his nostrils flared. "You!"

Before Joanie could respond, he pulled back his hand and struck the side of her head, driving her back onto the bed. Her vision blurred, and she grappled for Diana when she heard her scream. Gripping her head between her hands, her vision cleared in time to see Diana's fragile body careen across the room.

"No," Joanie shouted, ignoring her throbbing head. She would be damned before he laid another finger on Diana. Damned or dead. Crawling off the bed, she put herself once again between Geoffrey and Diana.

"You will not hurt her, not now, not anymore," Joanie shouted.

She closed her eyes as Geoffrey's hand pulled back again, but the pain never came.

She opened her eyes and found Simon holding Geoffrey's wrist from behind.

"Why do you do this?" Simon gasped.

Joanie's eyes widened. She had never heard Simon question the master before. He had always stood by when Geoffrey saw fit to punish them.

"Joanie dazzled them. She...she was celebrated. They adored her," Simon said.

"She defied me," Geoffrey thundered. "They both did."

He pushed past Joanie, toward Diana."

"No, Geoffrey. You mustn't," Simon implored.

Geoffrey's hand lashed out in a blur. A breath later, he had Simon's face pinched between his merciless fingers. "Stay out of this, Simon, as you've always done, or you will regret it."

Simon was the stronger man. Joanie held her breath, waiting, hoping for him to fight back, but his arms remained stiff at his sides. Still, he did not surrender. "You will kill her," he managed to say. Geoffrey looked Simon in the eye for several moments. Then he dropped his hand.

Simon rubbed his cheeks. "She is sick, gravely so."

Geoffrey turned, but he did not cross to where Diana lay sprawled out on the floor. Instead, he closed the distance between him and Joanie. She kept her head down, her heart racing. Then he crooked his thumb and gently lifted her chin. His soft gaze churned her stomach. She hated the admiration she saw in his eyes more than his fists. He turned her head from side to side, studying her. Then his eyes roamed over her figure before a slight smile curved his lips.

"My own hidden jewel. You will sing again tomorrow night, but this time — you sing for me." He dropped his hand to his side as he shifted his gaze to Diana. "You have two days to recover or else you are finished, and Joanie will take your place."

Then he turned on his heel and left the room, his guard, including Simon, falling in line behind him.

Chapter Eleven

Alec sat in the back of the great hall, his eyes trained on the high dais where Joanie stood elegantly dressed in a copper-colored tunic. Her raven black hair shone in waves that teased her narrow waist, and her white skin gleamed in the candlelight. A stirring melody, rich and sensual, poured forth from her full lips as she gazed above the heads of avid onlookers to a world unseen and unknown to anyone but her. Seduced by her slow, languid movements, the men within the hall ogled her as she wove among the trencher tables. They wanted to reach out and claim her for themselves, to pull her onto their laps and feel her body through her clothing. They wanted to own her, like a prize, something else to prove their greatness to the world.

She glided past them all, staying just out of reach. Then a flash caught Alec's eye. Geoffrey Mercer snaked his hand out, grabbing for Joanie's arm, but she twirled away just in time to escape his touch.

Once more, Alec felt her fear hurtle toward him. This combined with Geoffrey's sudden fury and the pulsing lust from the other men in the room, creating a turbulent storm of emotion within his heart and mind. Pressing both hands on the table, he stood, and watched Geoffrey's anger grow with every short breath he forced down his lungs.

The last note from Joanie's lips circled the ceiling of the great hall before its beauty drifted down to settle around the listeners in an echo of grace and vibrancy. The end of her song fueled Geoffrey's anger. He lunged to his feet, but enraptured onlookers stood between his fury and Joanie's terror, cheering, applauding, and vying for her attention. Alec narrowed his eyes as Geoffrey whispered something to one of his guards who then set off toward her, pushing through the crowd. When he reached her, his hand closed around her upper arm, and he pulled her toward Geoffrey, whose lips twisted into a greedy smile as she drew near.

Alec started toward them, his eyes never leaving Joanie's terrified face.

The guard thrust her at Geoffrey, and she fell onto his lap. Her fear and anger assaulted Alec's senses as Geoffrey stroked her cheek with his thick fingers. Then he pinned her face between his hands. She pushed against his chest, straining to lean away from his advancing kiss.

"Don't fight me," Geoffrey snarled, pulling his hand back.

Fury exploded within Alec when he realized Geoffrey's intention, and he lunged forward, grabbing Geoffrey's arm before he could strike Joanie. In that moment of contact, Geoffrey's soul was laid bare to him.

Pleading women, their faces tear-streaked and bloodied, assaulted Alec's mind. So many women, dozens, wearing the mark of Geoffrey's fists. Alec recognized the beauty, Diana. And then he saw her — Joanie — but not as she was in the hall, dressed in finery, but tattered and filthy. She did not plead. She did not cry. She withstood his fury and protected Diana. Pain, hot and furious, struck Alec as he absorbed every blow she had ever received from Geoffrey. Then his dream rose like a hazy fog in his mind — Joanie standing on the bridge, guarded by lions, sobbing, "Help us."

Alec growled. His fist shot up, catching Geoffrey beneath his chin, snapping his head back.

Alec's stance did not waver when Geoffrey stood up — fury pulsing through him. His eyes narrowed, boring deeper into Geoffrey's black soul.

"You shouldn't have done that," Geoffrey sneered, then motioned with a jerk of his hand toward his guards who lunged at Alec.

But Alec was faster. Before the guards finished taking their first step, the sword he had strapped to his back was unsheathed and the tip pressed to Geoffrey's neck. The very next moment, the guards unsheathed their own blades, all raised at Alec. He could feel the heat of the guards' eyes on his flesh and their hearts quickening at the prospect of spilling his blood.

Alec stared hard at Geoffrey. He could end his worthless life with just a flick of his wrist.

"Enough," a loud voice shouted.

The keeper stepped forward. His regal gait and bored posturing belied a casualness Alec knew he did not feel. Underneath his calm facade, Alec could feel the keeper's pulse racing. "That will be enough, gentlemen."

Sir Hugh Godfrey stood and raised his cup, sloshing the amber liquid on the table. "I believe I'm one of the few gently born men in the room," he said, his voice thick with drink.

The keeper cast him a surly look before turning to Geoffrey. "Call off your men."

"Not before he steps down," Geoffrey growled.

But Alec had no intention of backing down. He was too full of fury and Geoffrey's hate and the images of beaten women. But then his eldest brother's words came to him, Jack's words — we are thieves, not murderers.

Alec fought for control as a new storm began to churn within his heart. He was one of Scotland's secret rebels. They stole from wealthy English nobles and gave the riches to Scottish peasants in need. They delivered messages to advance the cause. They broke Scottish nobles out of English prisons — they did not kill for simple vengeance or the momentary pleasure it might bring.

Alec gritted his teeth. He wanted to resist the light. He wanted to refuse the honor his parents had instilled in him. The battle between his two competing desires raged on. Did he play God and smite Geoffrey from the earth? Or did he choose to be the better man? His gaze shifted from Geoffrey, searching for Joanie. She stood not far from him, beside a large man with thinning brown hair and a neatly trimmed beard, her face a picture of terror.

"Damn it," Alec spat, dropping his blade.

"Now, stand down," the keeper snapped at Geoffrey's guards. At once, the men backed away. But Alec knew what was coming. He didn't flinch as Geoffrey thrust his own blade to Alec's neck.

"Put down your weapon," John shouted, his cool facade gone.

Geoffrey's eyes darted to the keeper but then locked once more with Alec's. "You saw what he did. He attacked me without provocation. Yet you defend him."

John shook his head. "I think not. I'm partial to that man, as you well know. I'd rather you not kill him."

"Then I demand he be flogged and thrown into the dungeon, or have you forgotten who I am, who I know, and whose coin now lines your purse?"

The keeper shrugged. "It's not just your coin that fills my purse." John turned to one of his own guards. "Bring me the girl. She seems to be at the heart of this altercation."

Alec closed his eyes for a moment, rebuilding his shields and chasing away the images of Joanie's suffering from his mind. He needed to hold fast to his control. Then he opened his eyes and watched as the keeper's guard gently took Joanie by the arm. At first, she resisted, but he whispered something in her ear that seemed to bring her calm, and she followed. When she was presented to the keeper, she dipped in a low curtsy.

"What is your name?" John asked.

"Joanie," she replied, her shoulders inching up closer to her ears.

"Just Joanie. Have you another name?"

"Joanie Picard," she said quietly, her head down.

"She is of my house, the house of Mercer," Geoffrey thundered. "My servant."

The keeper looked at Geoffrey with surprise. "Interesting. You've had this gem in your household and yet you have kept her to yourself all this time."

"Until recently she has been my leman's maid."

"Ah, yes, the beautiful Diana," John said as he eyed Joanie. Alec could feel the keeper's mounting lust.

"It would seem you purchased a servant, but I do not see a servant standing before me. I see a prize." Then John turned to Geoffrey. "Let me help you settle this matter. I will buy the girl off your hands."

Alec could feel Joanie's heart pound harder as her eyes widened. She stepped away from the keeper, but he reached out and took her hand. "Look! She blushes like a maid."

"She's not for sale," Geoffrey snapped, lunging for Joanie, but the keeper's guards blocked his way.

John didn't respond to Geoffrey's refusal. Instead, he quietly studied Joanie. "I'll give you ten marks," he said softly, reaching out to stroke her cheek, but Joanie cringed and shrank away.

"Do not insult me," Geoffrey growled.

"Twenty marks then."

Fear, anger, and humiliation pulsed from Joanie's broken heart as the men haggled for her life.

Alec stepped forward. "I will give you one-hundred silver marks."

Joanie gasped when she heard the sum from Randolph's lips, and so did everyone else in the room. Then a hush settled over the hall. Joanie watched as Alec and Geoffrey stared at each other. Geoffrey's face was red with fury, and his hands were clenched in tight fists. Meanwhile, Randolph stood with his now familiar grace, his tall, sinewy body leaning against one of the trencher tables, his expression as unreadable as ever.

Her mind raced. One-hundred silver marks could purchase a household of servants. Geoffrey could keep a harem of mistresses in luxury for a year with such a sum.

"For pity's sake," the keeper said. "If you are waiting for a better offer from me, you will not have one. Take this fool's money, Geoffrey, before he comes to his senses."

Geoffrey's gaze flitted between Joanie and Alec and the keeper. Then he reached out his hand to Alec. "She's yours," he snarled.

Alec looked at Geoffrey's hand, but he did not accept it. Instead, he strode around Geoffrey to Joanie's side, taking hold of her arm. Joanie stiffened at his touch.

"Not until I have my coin," Geoffrey snapped.

John nodded. "He is right, Randolph. Release her and fetch the promised coin."

Joanie could feel the heat pouring off her new owner as he stared daggers at her old master. Then he turned to the keeper. "Have your guard escort Joanie to her room." He cut his eyes sidelong at Geoffrey. "Have them wait outside for my arrival." Then he looked at her. Despite the heat coming from his body in waves into her soul, his eyes held no warmth. His hollow expression sent chills up her spine. "I will come to you in an hour's time. Be ready to leave the castle." Then he turned on his heel and strode from the hall.

Chapter Twelve

The keeper's guard opened Diana's door for Joanie. "Thank you," she muttered before the door closed behind her.

Diana lifted her head from her pillow. "You're whiter than usual," she rasped. "What happened?"

Joanie wandered aimlessly into the room, her arms hanging limp at her sides while her mind tried to navigate through a fog of disbelief.

"Joanie!" Diana burst out, cutting through Joanie's haze. "What has happened?"

"I've been sold," she said and slumped onto the bed.

Diana's eyes widened in horror. "To whom?"

Joanie's lips trembled. "To Randolph Tweed."

Diana gasped and sat up. "No! I won't allow it."

"It is done. He promised Geoffrey one-hundred silver marks."

"But that is a fortune! Why would he pay such a price?"

Joanie shook her head. "I dare not consider why. Anyway, the matter is arranged. It is done. He promised to come for me in an hour's time. I am supposed to be ready to leave the palace."

"But ... you can't leave me," Diana cried. "You—"

Joanie put her hand up to silence Diana. "Listen," she said, her heart pounding. Footfalls sounded in the hallway. "But I've only just returned. He cannot come for me now." Joanie clutched Diana's hand. "One of the keeper's own soldiers escorted me here and now guards the door. Mayhap, he will not be granted entry."

Just then the clanging of blades stung Joanie's ears, and a moment later something or someone slammed into the door and thudded to the ground. Deafening silence followed.

Diana wrapped her arms around Joanie. "I won't let him take you," she cried.

Then the door swung wide, and Simon thundered into the room.

Joanie looked past him at the crumpled body of the guard on the floor. "He's ... you ... you killed him."

Simon shook his head. "I only rendered him unconscious. I had to. How else could I save Diana?" He crossed the room and scooped Diana into his arms. Cradling her close, he pressed a long kiss to her brow.

"I'm glad you're here," Diana whispered, cupping Simon's face.

Joanie thought of all the times Simon had stood by and let Geoffrey beat them. "Why did you never interfere before?"

"Believe me, Joanie, it killed me to watch him hurt her and you, but she made me promise not to interfere."

Diana nodded, still staring up into Simon's eyes. "I told him that I would rather belong to the Devil and live in luxury, than be free and know poverty again."

Simon's mouth settled into a grim line. He set Diana back on the bed and stood. "But that time has come to an end." Then he turned to Joanie. "You both need to leave right now. Put together a satchel." Then he handed Joanie a heavy purse. "This coin will guarantee her comfort, but I need your word, Joanie. Promise me that you'll take care of her."

"Do not speak of me as if I am not here," Diana snapped. "As if I am already dead."

A wave of pain twisted Simon's features, but his gaze never left Joanie's. "Give me your word."

Joanie nodded. "I swear it. You know I will take care of her as I've always done. But why are you not coming with us?"

Simon shook his head. "I will stay behind and do what I must to keep him from following you."

Joanie hated the idea of Simon carrying on beneath Geoffrey's thumb. "Come with us," she urged. "Run with us. You deserve more than this life too."

Simon shook his head sadly and pulled Joanie into his arms. "Diana cannot run," he whispered in her ear. "She is not long for this world as you well know. You must take her to a hospital or an abbey where she can die in peace and with dignity — my coin will pay for her care and a proper burial."

"What is going on?" Diana asked.

Simon let go of Joanie. "It is time to go," he said, loud enough for Diana to hear.

Diana looked around the room nervously. "Please tell me what is going on."

Simon made no reply. Instead, he reached for Diana and helped her to her feet. "Can you walk?"

Joanie watched as Diana's white-knuckled grip on Simon's arm loosened, and she took her first tentative steps. Slowly, she straightened her spine and walked to the center of the room where she stopped, her stance regal. Joanie could see the glint in her eye — Diana would fight until the last breath fled her body. "I can walk," she gritted.

Simon turned to Joanie. "Are you ready?"

Joanie shook her head and set to work, packing a satchel for Diana. When she had her mistress's effects and the herbs and oils she would need, she nodded.

"I will take you as far as the kitchens," he said. "The keeper is lazy and arrogant. Only the front gates to the palace are guarded. You can leave through the gardens. Stick to the palace wall. There is a gate on the far right. On the other side, you will find passage across the Thames."

"Please come with us," Joanie said, trying to reason with Simon one last time, but he cut her off.

"Enough," he snapped. "Now, stay close. Remain silent until you are on the other side of the river."

Joanie hastened to the door while Simon escorted Diana, bearing her proudly on his arm.

When they descended the stairs to the kitchen and stepped out into the garden, Simon cupped Diana's cheeks. "With angels trumpeting we will meet again," he said, and then he kissed her.

Tears flooded Joanie's eyes as she watched Diana lean into Simon's kiss, her lips trembling, her hands desperately gripping his tunic. A gasp of longing reached Joanie's ears, and in that moment, she realized that Diana did, indeed, return Simon's love.

Chapter Thirteen

Joanie gripped the sides of the small boat as they made their way across the Thames. Her threadbare hood offered little protection from the icy wind. Diana sat in front of her. Despite her thick cloak and the numerous veils Joanie had wrapped around her face with just her eyes visible to the night, Diana still coughed. But they were quickly approaching the other side of the river. Joanie eyed the docks, which were eerily quiet in the cold night.

The last time she had stood on the docks, London's riverport had been bustling with merchants and passengers. The palace had soared above the river, awe-inspiring against the bright sky. She dared to glance back, past the downcast head of the river man, at the palace looming now in shadowy darkness. She thought of Geoffrey and prayed she would never see her master again. And then she remembered, she had a new master. Would he search for her? At the price of one-hundred silver marks, Joanie could not imagine that Randolph Tweed would simply let her go. Fear began to mount in her mind, but she straightened her back and pushed concerns for herself away. She needed to find a hospital quickly. What little strength Diana still possessed would soon be exhausted.

After the boatman assisted both Diana and Joanie onto shore, she straightened Diana's veils and pulled the rich fur cloak tighter around her shoulders. At the very least, Diana looked as fine as any lady Joanie had glimpsed from afar, and she looked like Diana's maid. Their pretense of status, she prayed would protect them as they started down the dark narrow dirt streets. Motley pedestrians eyed them with interest; still, to Joanie's great relief, they cleared the docks without incident.

Icy patches slowed their progress as they left the riverbank and headed further into the city. They passed clay and thatch homes and narrow alleys, dotted with fire pits where people warmed their hands. After years of being sequestered in Diana's room, only to leave when Geoffrey's household changed abode, Joanie was struck by the din and inescapable smells.

"Stand up straight," Diana said. "You are trying to hide inside yourself again. Put your shoulders down. Your fear will draw trouble like a moth to flame."

Joanie stood straight and tried to mirror Diana's stride. Diana moved like a queen, but upon closer inspection her breath rattled and was coming in shorter and quicker gasps. "I'm sorry, Joanie. I ... I do not know how much farther I can go."

"Look there," Joanie exclaimed, pointing to a church up ahead. "Surely someone there can help us."

The double doors leading into the church were locked. "There must be another door," Joanie said.

"At this hour, it is likely to be locked as w—" Diana said, her words overtaken by a vicious cough.

Joanie wrapped her arm around Diana's waist. "If I asked you to leave me here on the steps, I'm guessing you would refuse me," Diana said, a weak chuckle escaping her bluish lips.

"We are almost there," Joanie said. She spied the door up ahead. It, too, was locked. Joanie banged on the wood with her fist. Again and again, she beat the door, unwilling to accept defeat.

"There is no point," Diana said, leaning her head against Joanie's legs as she continued to pound on the door.

"I will not give up," Joanie cried, her fist sore. Then suddenly she heard movement coming from inside the church, and a moment later, the door opened a crack. A priest with a deeply furrowed brow held a lamp high. He glared at Joanie through the crack, but when he noticed Diana his expression softened.

"My lady," he said, opening the door fully. Diana smiled her beautiful smile and accepted the priest's hand.

"Thank you, Father," she said. She stood and stepped into the stone hallway. Torch fire cast dancing shadows on the walls. Joanie followed Diana inside, her eyes drawn to the high arched ceilings.

"My lady, why have you come to me?"

"I..." Diana's hand flew to her head the instant before she slumped in the priest's arms.

He gathered her close to him and felt her brow. "She burns like fire."

Joanie nodded. "She is gravely ill. She needs a bed."

The priest raised his brows. "Where is her family? We are a humble parish. I cannot take her in."

Joanie raised Simon's heavy purse. "I have coin. Your parish will be greatly rewarded for this kindness."

The priest hesitated at the sight of the purse. He considered Diana a moment longer before he nodded. "I am Father Ambrose. You are both welcome. I will do all I can for her."

The priest scooped Diana into his arms, cradling her. Joanie followed him through the empty chapel, which was shrouded in shadow. Beyond the sacristy, he asked Joanie to open a large door, which led into a narrow, stone hallway with a high arched ceiling. She stepped aside, letting Father Ambrose enter first. After passing several doors, he stopped in front of one and glanced at Joanie. "It is unlocked."

She nodded and stepped in front of him, opening the door. They were greeted by darkness. Undeterred, Father Ambrose walked headlong into the dark with Diana in his arms.

"Bring me one of the candles from the hall," he said.

When she returned, the single flame illuminated a small room with naught but a straw mattress on the floor, a rough-hewn table and chair and another smaller table in the corner with a basin and pitcher.

He laid Diana on the mattress, then he stood and turned to Joanie. "Rest for now. In the morning, we will discuss what must be done."

"Thank you, Father," Joanie said before the door closed.

She turned on her feet, taking in the small room, and then she looked down at Diana. Her face looked peaceful as she slept, but her raspy breaths panged Joanie's heart. In that moment, she realized there was naught else she could do but lie down on the floor next to Diana and surrender to sleep.

ALEC HEADED TOWARD the southern wing. Handing Geoffrey Mercer the large purse without drawing his blade and running him through had been the greatest test of Alec's self-control. The greedy, smug look that lit Geoffrey's eyes when he clutched the bag to his chest still twisted Alec's stomach. The one consolation to which Alec clung was the knowledge of how Geoffrey would suffer once Alec stole the coin back. But that could wait. First, he was going to bring Joanie to a safe place, far from the palace and out of reach of Geoffrey's punishing fists.

The southern wing stretched out in front of him. Straightaway, his eyes narrowed on the guard sprawled out on the floor in front of one of the doors. He raced forward, stepping over the unconscious man, throwing open the door. The room was empty, but he knew it had been Diana's, not just by the finery scattered about the room, the oils and perfumes — he could feel Joanie's presence.

But where was she now?

Again, he saw her, so clearly, standing on the bridge, her heart and soul pleading for his.

He stormed from the room. So many questions plagued his heart. He had but one certitude — he knew where he would find her. When he did find her, he only prayed that she was not as desolate as in his vision.

Chapter Fourteen

"Good morrow," Joanie heard Diana whisper. Although awake, Joanie had yet to open her eyes. Diana's green eyes slowly came into focus as Joanie searched for the strength and courage to face the day. In the end, it was the purple circles beneath Diana's eyes that brought her fully wake.

"How are you feeling this morning?" Joanie asked as she sat up.

Diana smiled slightly. "Do you really need to ask?"

Joanie stood and grabbed her heavy satchel, searching for soothing herbs.

"What are you doing?" Diana asked.

Not looking up, Joanie said, "I am going to make your morning tisane. Then I will mix a fresh plaster for your chest, and—"

"Joanie," Diana said, interrupting.

This time she looked up. "What it is?"

"Why do you bother?"

"Whatever do you mean?"

"I'm dying," she said softly. "Why not let me die?"

"Don't talk like that," Joanie scolded. Then she turned back to her herbs. "I need more Horehound. I will ask Father Ambrose for some."

Diana shook her head. "We have bothered the good father enough. It must be late enough for the markets to be up. Why don't you go and buy what you need?"

Joanie considered her limited supply. She had been rushed the night before; there were several important herbs she had been remiss in packing. "Will you be all right without me?"

"No," Diana said, tears stinging her eyes. "How could I ever get on without you, Joanie?" She swept a trembling hand across her wet cheeks and took a deep breath. "But in the end, I know I will be just fine." Then she pointed to the table. "Take Simon's purse. There is more than enough there to buy whatever it is you might need."

Joanie reached for the purse and plucked out two coins. "This will be enough." Then she swept her tattered cloak around her shoulders. "Is there anything in particular you would like?" Joanie asked.

"Your forgiveness," Diana said.

Joanie's eyes widened. "Forgiveness? Whatever for?"

Diana closed her eyes. "We all need forgiveness every now and then. None of us are perfect." Then she looked up at Joanie and smiled. "Even if we would like to be remembered that way."

Joanie returned her smile. "I think you should rest a while longer." She bent and pressed a kiss to Diana's cheek. "I will speak to the priest before I leave to ensure he checks in on you."

"I'm sure he will," Diana said. Then she turned and curled up on the bed facing the wall. "I love you, Joanie."

"I love you too," Joanie whispered, softly closing the door as she left.

Chapter Fifteen

The buildings lining the narrow streets blurred as tears flooded Joanie's eyes. She pulled her cloak tighter around her chin to block out the chill. Large snowflakes drifted down, sashaying through the air and settling on the dirt roads and rundown buildings like an icing of frosty lace to cover the drab thatch roofs. Her stomach rumbled as she passed by a vendor with baked apples and warm mead bubbling in a pot. Snowflakes found the hot surface and disappeared the instant they touched down in the boiling drink.

The man eyed her distastefully. "Unless you've a hay penny in your pocket to buy a sip, you just keep on walking."

Joanie scurried away. She didn't have a hay penny or any other penny for that matter.

Two days prior, when she had returned to the chapel from the market, the priest had refused her entry...

"I'm sorry, my child, but she does not want you here," Father Ambrose said gently.

Joanie stiffened. "What are you talking about?"

"Your mistress told me not to grant you entry."

"You're lying," Joanie said, barreling up the stairs. But Father Ambrose and two servants who flanked his sides barred the way. She tried to shove past them. "Diana," she shouted, pushing her face through his arms. "Diana!"

The priest's servants, two strong, young men, grabbed her arms and dragged her backward down the steps. Her heart pounded. She could hardly draw breath. "Let me go! She needs me!"

"This is not my doing. This is your mistress's will," Father Ambrose said, his brows drawn together.

Joanie shook her head, the priest's sympathetic face blurred as tears flooded her eyes. "I don't believe you," she sobbed, trying to yank her arms free. "Please, don't do this. She needs me."

Father Ambrose clasped his hands as if in prayer and descended the steps. "She wanted me to give you this message. She does not want you to watch her waste away and die. She wants you to remember her as she always was, beautiful and strong. Also, she wants you to take yourself far from here, away from London."

"No," Joanie cried, covering her ears with her hands. Her stomach twisted. The sour taste of bile filled her mouth.

"And she wanted me to give you this." From beneath his robe, Father Ambrose produced a small purse. "I have kept for the parish what I require for her care and burial. She bade me give you the remainder."

Joanie gaped in horror at the purse. She shook her head. "Please, Father, she is not well. She ... she does not know what she is doing."

Father Ambrose canted his head to the side, his expression soft. "You love her dearly, I can see. I am so sorry for your loss."

"But she isn't dead," Joanie screamed as she rushed the stairs. But one of the servants thrust his arm out, knocking her back. The back of her head slammed against the ground.

"Be gentle with her." She heard Father Ambrose snap over the ringing that filled her ears.

"Are you all right?" he asked, his face suddenly looming above hers. He laid his hand on her head. "I will do everything in my power to see that she does not suffer."

Heartache twisted the pit of her stomach. "Please," she cried, her hands covering her face.

The servants helped her stand. Her head pounded.

"Take this," she heard the priest say.

She glanced at the purse in his hand. She waved it away with a feeble gesture. "That was not intended for me."

Father Ambrose seized her arm. "Do not be a fool. Take the coin."

She pressed her lips together, fighting her tears. "Release me now," she gritted. When the pressure from her arm vanished. She took a step back. Then without looking up she whispered, "Tell her I love her," before she turned and stumbled down the street.

Joanie reached behind her head. Blood still oozed from a gash on the back of her head when she fell off the stairs. The wetness around her hair and cloak had frozen in the cold. She ripped her tunic into strips, wadding one up to soak up the blood and securing it to the wound with the other. After tying off the knot, she pulled her hood low over her head. She hunched over, trying to escape the blustery wind as she continued down the narrow road. She knew not where she was going. She was desperate for food, and never had she known such cold. Glancing down, she could see that her feet still moved, but they were completely numb. And she wondered whether she was still truly walking or was she dreaming her worst nightmare yet. Then Diana's words returned to her. *There are worse pains than the might of a fist. Hunger. Cold. Those are the real demons.*

When Diana had spoken those words, Joanie had not believed her. She could not imagine facing anything worse than Geoffrey's temper, but that was pain she had been able to fight against, hide from. The hunger that gripped her belly and the cold that slowed her steps could not be outrun, or slapped away, or hidden from. They could not be ignored by a secret place inside of her.

Up ahead, she spied a fire pit. She kept her eyes on the dancing flames and forced her feet to walk one in front of the other. She felt the warmth even from a distance, enticing her stiff limbs to speed up, and then, suddenly, she stood next to the blazing heat, warming her hands over the licking flames. Needles of pain stabbed her fingers as feeling began to return.

"Get away from there," a woman shouted, coming at her with a broom. "That is heating up for my laundry. It's not for trash like you." Then a dog came from around her skirts, barking and gnashing its teeth. Fear pulsed through Joanie, and she ran, her heart pounding in her ears. The woman's hateful voice and the bark of the dog followed her, filling her mind, pushing her ever faster although she knew she had long outrun the threat.

At last, she collapsed, her mind still reeling, but her body had surrendered. It would take her no further. People from all walks of life and stations strode past her, giving her a wide berth. Through a haze, she watched them avert their eyes, ignoring her need. Snow danced down and her eyes followed the rhythm, which slowly grew faster as the snow thickened into a gauzy curtain, obscuring the buildings and passersby. As darkness approached, the wind picked up, blasting her face with ice and snow.

One side of the street still bustled with people, hunched over, escaping the storm. On the other side, there was a bridge guarded by two ferocious stone lions. People rushed to cross over to the other side. She rolled over onto her stomach, searching for what lay beneath the bridge. A deep ditch only dusted with snow and out of reach of the wind's sharp talons, beckoned her. Crawling down the banking, she scrambled for cover, and finally collapsed onto her back. She angled her head to peer around the wrought iron, her eyes following one snowflake's descent to the ground. Everything else had gone away, except the cold winter sky, black but full of power. She stared upward, feeling no pain, no cold, no fear, no joy. She was nameless, her mind and heart empty. Shadows closed in on her vision, and she welcomed the approaching oblivion. A breath away from what felt like her last, a face suddenly intruded upon her nothingness. Eyes as black and cold as the winter night sky looked down at her. Long black hair swept her skin when he drew closer. He was beautiful and somehow familiar. Strong arms enclosed her, lifting her away from the cold ground. He pressed her close, wrapping his cloak around her. Warmth immediately surrounded her, reaching her soul-deep. It was as if he had lit a fire within her body, heating her from the inside out. And yet when she met his gaze a chill crept up her fiery spine.

"Are you an angel or the devil?" she whispered.

He looked down at her. His face remained unchanged. "I am just a man." Despite his aloof tone, his voice was deep and unhurried and fueled the fire that continued to warm her body.

She curled deeper into his arms. "Liar," she whispered. And then the world faded away into a dreamy haze.

Chapter Sixteen

Alec cradled Joanie close. His arms enveloped her, her body pressed tightly to his, and yet he sensed nothing. Never had he known the pleasure of simply holding a woman in his arms. In the past, whenever he had held a woman close, he had also embraced her emotions and memories. But not with Joanie.

Still, habit and caution bade that when he entered the Anchor tavern and followed Moira into one of the rooms upstairs, he laid Joanie on the bed and immediately stepped back, putting distance between them.

"For pity's sake, Alec, do not be so hard," Moira scolded before turning to stroke Joanie's cheek. "Poor wee lamb." Then she looked back to Alec. "Help me remove her cloak and turn her so I can see the wound better."

Alec did not step forward. The stone around his neck blazed against his chest, which only added to his confusion. Why did the stone respond to her? He stared at the creature on the bed who was such a mystery to him.

Moira put her hands on her hips. In her anger, her true Scottish brogue came out. "Ye heard me, Alec MacVie. I know there's a beating heart somewhere in that body. What little compassion ye have, ye may want to spend on her." Then she cocked a brow at him. "Unless ye want me to bring one of the lassies in to help."

Alec cocked a brow back at Moira. There was no way he was going to let anyone else in the room. He took a deep breath, then reached for Joanie. Untying her cloak, he lifted her and set her upright on his lap, letting her head rest against his chest. He closed his eyes, waiting, expectant, but again nothing came to his mind. Lulled by her quiet soul, he leaned against the wall and listened to the steady beating of her heart. All he felt was peace — no chaos, no revealing truths or hidden deceptions — only peace. He watched Moira's expert hands quickly and gently cleanse and dress the gash on Joanie's head.

"'Tis done," Moira said. "Ye can lay her back down."

Which Alec did ... eventually. But first he stayed there in that spot and held her, savoring the peaceful rhythm of her heart and breath.

JOANIE STRUGGLED TO open her eyes. Slowly, the room came into focus. A fire burned brightly in the hearth. She stared at the dancing flames. Then her eye caught a movement near the foot of her bed. She sucked in a sharp breath and scurried against the wall as she met Randolph Tweed's hard, emotionless face. He said nothing but stood and moved his seat away from the bed next to the hearth where he continued to stare at her.

She didn't know what to say or how to explain her running away. Was he vexed? Was he trying to frighten her? She just wished he would say something. Finally, she could handle the silence no longer. She blurted out, "Master Randolph—"

But he cut her off before she could say another word. "My name is Alec MacVie. And I am not yer master."

A thick Scottish brogue shaped his words. She stared at him dumbstruck. "You're Scottish?" she asked hesitantly.

"Aye, is that a problem?"

Who was this man?

He stared at her for some time, not speaking. When he did speak, she jumped.

"Moira will be in with food for ye." He stood up and looked down at her. "She will lock the door behind her when she leaves to make sure ye don't decide to run off again."

"You are leaving?"

"Aye. The coin I paid for ye wasn't mine — it's Scotland's money. I'm going to get it back."

Her eyes widened. "Geoffrey is not just going to return your money."

Alec looked at her. If she didn't know better, she might have thought a smile played at his lips. "I wasn't planning on asking him," he said.

Her eyes widened. "Do you mean you are going to steal it?"

He shrugged. "Wouldn't be the first time."

He crossed once more to her side. He was so still, his face unreadable, but she felt him like fire inside of her. She knew he wanted to say something or do something, but he held back.

"Moira will see to yer comfort," he said, then he turned and left without a backward glance.

Joanie's jaw hung slack as she stared at the door. She did not know what to think. But she was warm, and for that she was grateful. A few minutes later, a woman with a bright, pretty face and lovely red hair came into the room.

"Good morrow" she beamed. "My name is Mary. Do not fret, Randolph will return shortly."

Joanie shot the woman a glance then turned back to look at the fire, wrapping her arms around her knees. "He told me his real name."

"Did he now?" Moira's surprised tone also carried a Scottish brogue. She smiled when Joanie looked up. "If he trusts ye enough to give ye his Christian name, then I suppose I should do the same. Ye can call me, Moira, lass."

Joanie pulled her knees tighter to her chest and started to rock.

"Ye don't need to be so nervous, Joanie. Ye can trust me."

"Why are you in London then, pretending to be English?" Joanie blurted.

Moira shook her head but smiled kindly. "Now if Alec has not yet enlightened ye on that count, I will follow his lead and hold my tongue." Moira cocked her head to one side as she looked down at Joanie with kind, warm eyes. "Ye needn't be frightened, love. No one is going to hurt ye. I don't yet know Alec's interest in ye or what his plans are, but I tell ye for certain that he will keep ye safe from whatever danger ye're in."

Joanie stiffened. "What makes you think I'm in danger?"

"A wee lass like yerself shows up in the arms of Alec MacVie, bleeding and unconscious, I'm going to have to assume she's met with trouble. And from what I know of trouble, it doesn't go away so easily."

Joanie looked away and stared back at the fire. Moira was right about that. Trouble had followed Joanie her whole life.

Moira sat next to her and swept back a lock of hair that had fallen in front of Joanie's eyes. "I brought ye some soup and some bread," she said in a soft voice. "Come sit with me by the hearth and try to eat a little."

Joanie looked at the broth and crusty bread but felt no desire to eat. She had long since moved beyond hunger to numb emptiness. How could she eat when despair laid claim to her heart? Tears stung her eyes, and she looked away, hiding her face from Moira.

Moira's arm came around her comfortingly. "What is it, love?"

Joanie sniffed and swiped at her tears, shaking her head.

"Ye'll feel better if ye tell me."

"I don't want to feel better," Joanie snapped. "Not when Diana suffers so."

Moira continued to stroke Joanie's hair, and when she spoke her soothing tone was unaltered by Joanie's outburst. "Who is Diana, and why does she suffer?"

After several moments passed, Joanie finally turned to look at Moira. "She is my mistress." Her lips trembled. She swallowed the hard knot in her throat so that the remainder of her words could get out. "And she is dying. Even as I speak, she could be slipping from this world."

Moira's eyes widened. She placed her hand on Joanie's. "Where is she? I will take ye to her myself."

Tears blurred the fire into watery orange streaks. "She sent me away. She didn't want me to stay with her. She wanted me to get away from London, away from our master." Then she paused and looked at Moira. "Away from Randolph too ... I mean Alec."

Moira pulled her into her arms and rocked her. "She wants to protect ye then."

Joanie could not answer. Instead, she allowed Moira to hold her and nodded through her tears.

"If her time is not long for this world, then what would matter most to her is not herself but those she leaves behind, namely ye, Joanie."

Joanie knew Moira was right. She knew that Diana had only been thinking of Joanie's wellbeing when she sent her away. Joanie let the dam holding back her emotions break as she buried herself deeper in Moira's arms. Moira continued to rock her and say soothing words like her grandmother used to say to her. *There, there, wee lamb. Ye just cry all ye want, sweetling.*

After a while, with no more tears left to cry, she sat up and wiped her eyes. Immediately, her gaze was drawn to the large wet mark on Moira's tunic. "Forgive me. I should not have carried on so." She shrunk away closer to the wall, but Moira grabbed her hand, ensuring she could not go far.

"Hush now. None of that nonsense. Ye've been through a great deal." Moira reached out and cupped Joanie's cheek and softly said, "And judging by those big, wounded eyes, I've barely glimpsed the dark shadows that haunt ye."

Joanie didn't know what to say. She was not accustomed to compassion.

Moira smiled, and Joanie allowed her to pull her to her feet, lulled by her kindness.

"I'm starving," Moira said. "Ye'd be doing me a favor if ye'd sit and break yer fast with me."

Joanie did as she was bid. She could not deny Moira after she had been so kind. She sat in the chair and curled her knees into her chest. She didn't like chairs. She had always felt so vulnerable with her feet on the ground, and her soft underbelly exposed. She preferred the floor where she could fold her knees into her chest. She nibbled on the bread and stared into the flames. Allowing her mind to empty, she surrendered to numbness.

After their meal, Moira left and returned several minutes later with a basket of mending. She set it on the floor near the table and took out a tunic in need of hemming.

Joanie eyed the basket. "May I?" she asked, glancing across the table at Moira.

A sad smile curved Moira's lips, but then her smile grew, and she nodded, her lovely red curls bouncing. "We're kindred spirits, ye and I," she said. "I can't sit with idle hands either."

Blushing, Joanie lowered her head, hiding her gaze from Moira's. Then she snaked her hand out and quickly grabbed a folded length of linen from the top of the pile. With new purpose, she unfolded her legs and reached for a needle.

Two hours later, with a neat pile of newly mended clothing, Joanie set her needle down and stretched her arms over her head just as the door swung open. Alec had to dip his head when he entered. His long hair framed his face, falling below his chest on either side. Her heart started to pound when his black eyes met hers.

"We have to go," he said. Then he shut the door behind him and began to gather his few belongings, stuffing them into the satchel he wore crossed over his torso.

His face remained impassive, but the hurried motions of his hands belied his emotionless facade.

Joanie stood. "Where are we going?"

Alec shook his head. "There is no time," he said, his voice hard.

"Were ye not able to get the money back?" Moira asked, standing.

Alec shook his head. "I have Scotland's money. The fool Geoffrey left the bag in clear sight in his room, too drunk on ale and fury to protect what was his." He gestured to Joanie, "which is not surprising, considering his lack of care for his servants."

"What is it then?" Moira asked, her voice rising with the concern and emotion that Alec's own tone refused to betray.

"A legion of Edward's knights rode through the palace gates as I was leaving."

Moira's eyes widened. "Do you think he knows about the robbery?"

Alec nodded. "I know he does. The keeper sent word about the stolen treasure a fortnight ago. We all should leave London."

Joanie's head darted from Alec to Moira as she listened closely to their exchange. She did not understand much of what they spoke of, but she could tell by Moira's tone that Alec had brought ill news. Still, he himself could have been speaking on any subject — the cold weather, a list of chores that needed doing. Listening to his emotionless voice, no one would have guessed he spoke of the return of kings and stolen treasure.

"Close the inn. And spread the word. I want all of Scotland's agents out of London by tonight." Then he strode over to Joanie and took her by the forearm. "We are leaving."

She tugged her arm free, afraid of the black eyes staring down at her. "Can I stay with Moira?"

But with a shake of his head, he shattered her hopes. She looked at Moira, hoping Moira would champion her, but she only shook her head.

"Nay, lass. 'Tis too dangerous. Stay with Alec. He'll protect ye."

Alec took hold of her forearm again. Joanie looked at the resolute expression Moira wore and knew she would not yield to Joanie's pleas. She turned and looked at Alec. His shoulders, although not overly broad, were strong, just like the rest of him. She knew it was pointless to struggle, and so surrendered, allowing him to lead her from the inn.

Chapter Seventeen

Lord Aldrich Paxton stormed into the great hall of the king's palace, a band of twenty knights following at his heels. His eyes were drawn first to the high dais, left empty just as the king had commanded.

"At least the keeper did something right," he muttered under his breath. Then his eyes dropped to a trencher table at the fore of the room where a dozen richly dressed men now stood at his approach. Moving to the center of the room, each man knelt on one knee and bowed his head.

"Stand," Lord Paxton commanded when he reached the keeper and his cronies, not trying to conceal the disdain in his voice. "Which one of you is John Bigge?"

The man in question stood but kept his head downcast. Lord Paxton circled around him. "How well-ordered the hall appears," he said, making a sweeping gesture with his arms. "Where are your drunken companions now? Where are your whores?" He drew close to John and hissed in his ear. "Word reached Edward of the state of his palace, of the philanderers and villains who have roamed his halls and fornicated on his floors."

"My ... my lord," the keeper stammered.

"Silence," Aldrich shouted. Then he turned his back to the group and moved several feet away while he fought to control his temper. He had been taught that any expression of emotion was weakness, even when in the right.

After several moments, during which he knew the keeper and the other men likely grew increasingly nervous, Aldrich turned back around. "Word of the disastrous order you have kept reached Edward not two days before your message about the robbery of the Chapter House." Aldrich closed the distance to stand in front of the keeper. "Do you have any idea what you've allowed? The theft of holy relics and priceless royal treasure," he shouted in the keeper's face, answering his own question. He swung back around, showing his back once more to the men.

"I have sent many of the king's guards who remained here to recover the treasure," the keeper said in a quiet voice.

Aldrich turned back around. "By my command, Edward's soldiers have spread throughout the city and countryside with orders to drag the rivers and ponds and to search merchant stores, fresh graves and every hayloft from Dover to Cape Wrath. I do not doubt that the treasure will be recovered. Meanwhile, I have ordered the palace guards to return while I continue to investigate you, Keeper John Bigge." He scanned the men standing behind the keeper. "And the rest of you. You are all under house arrest. You and your households are to remain inside the palace until we have recovered the treasure and found the guilty parties. And in case you are all too dimwitted or still drunk from your revelries to understand my full meaning, allow me to state the obvious — you are all suspects in the theft of the Chapter House treasure."

The men gaped at him with eyes wide. "You are all merchants?" he asked, eying their garb, absorbing their stances and expressions. He considered himself a good judge of character, and despite the apparent wealth of each man, not one held true honor in his eyes. They were all thieves and sinners at heart, men who lacked the conviction needed to fight for justice or truth. These were not servants of God or protectors of the crown. These were men who served themselves alone.

He gestured to the long trencher table they had initially occupied. "Sit down," he snapped.

The men spread out along the benches while Aldrich removed his cloak, gesturing for one of the guards to take it. He laid his helmet and gauntlets on the table. Smoothing a wayward lock of red hair from his eyes, he ran his hand down his beard before he sat down at the head of the table. Folding his hands, he continued to consider the group, sizing up each man.

"'Tis simple, really," he began. "I am going to give you all the opportunity to supply me with what you know, specifically the names of guilty persons. Now, before you decide to keep your own confidence, I would like to remind you that you are all the king's prisoners and will remain so until this matter has been satisfactorily resolved."

"Jonathan," he said, looking to where a scribe stood among the warriors and gestured for the small man to join them. Jonathan's roughly-made brown tunic grazed the floor when he hurried over. Without a word, he reached into the satchel hanging across his chest and withdrew a piece of parchment, a jar of ink, and a quill. When he finished assembling what he needed, he nodded to Aldrich to signal he was ready.

Aldrich then turned to the group. "Would anyone like to give me a name?"

Without hesitation, the keeper spoke up. "Richard Ash."

Scratching of pen to parchment dominated the room for a moment as Jonathan scribbled the name.

"Go on," Aldrich said, looking expectantly at the keeper.

"He is your man, Richard Ash. Isn't that right?" The keeper asked, scanning the surrounding men for support. A murmur of quiet agreement echoed his plea.

"Yes."

"That's right."

"He's the one."

Aldrich raised his brow. "And how do you know Richard Ash is the guilty party? Did he confess his crime?"

The keeper shook his head. "Of course not, for I would have brought him to task and even now he would be chained in the dungeons below."

"If this Richard did not confess, then how do you know he did it?"

"He boasted of his plan one evening, but none of us took him at his word. He was drunk and a braggart, not to mention a dimwitted sort of man. No one believed he would act on his plan. Then after months of spending his evenings here at the palace, he suddenly disappeared. That same week, we discovered the stolen treasure. Only then did we realize that Richard must have carried out his foolhardy plan."

Jonathan turned to the scribe at his side. "Have a likeness done of Richard Ash. We will bring him in for questioning." Then Jonathan looked back to the keeper. "I assume you have sent out members of the guard to locate Richard."

The keeper straightened in his seat. "I certainly have, and you can question the guard to hear the truth, for that matter, although they've been unable to find him."

"It would appear as though this Richard was not as foolhardy as you all initially judged for him to pull off such a heist."

The men murmured their agreement. Aldrich resisted rolling his eyes as he considered the fools surrounding him. "Despite Richard's apparent cleverness, I am confident he did not act alone." Once more he scanned the group, looking every man in the eye. "So, which one of you helped him?"

The keeper's eyes grew wide. "One of us?"

Aldrich's fist came down on the table. The men visibly jumped in their seats. "Do not play me for the fool. He did not act alone. Tell me what you know."

"Randolph Tweed helped him," said a large man with black hair and a neatly trimmed beard.

Aldrich looked down the line of men and locked eyes with the man. "What is your name?"

"Geoffrey Mercer, I am a merchant."

"And you've been enjoying the king's hospitality for some time, have you not?"

He nodded. "I have, sir."

"What is the man's name you gave?"

"Randolph Tweed. He and Richard used to dine together. He's a knave and a proven thief too. He robbed me of a servant and one-hundred silver marks."

Aldrich looked to the other men. "Do you agree with Geoffrey? Do you believe this Randolph is guilty?"

The keeper hesitated for a moment. Aldrich did not miss the look exchanged between him and Geoffrey, but then the keeper nodded. "Yes, Randolph and Richard were close. I do not doubt he knew of Richard's plan, and more than likely aided him."

Aldrich nodded, then turned to the scribe. "Have a likeness done of this Randolph Tweed as well." He stood then. "You are all dismissed to your rooms where you will remain until you are told otherwise."

"If it pleases my Lord Paxton, I will volunteer my time and my men to help track down these villains."

Jonathan turned and eyed Geoffrey. He was a large man, and judging by his attire, he was a successful merchant. No doubt he could afford capable men. "Are your men trained for battle?"

Geoffrey nodded. "And they can ride as well as any knight. What's more, the head of my guard is a skilled tracker."

Jonathan raised his brows. "Is that so?" He gestured to one of his men. "Evaluate this man's guard. If you deem them worthy, add another twenty cavalry to his party." Then he turned back to Geoffrey. "Allowing you meet with my man's approval, I accept your aid on behalf of the king."

Jonathan saw the unmistakable glint of vengeance in Geoffrey's eye. "Whatever this Randolph has done to you, remember your first interest is to the crown."

"Randolph Tweed will stand in front of King Edward in irons," Geoffrey said, bowing his head. "You have my word."

Chapter Eighteen

Alec held Joanie's hand and pulled her just behind him, keeping her close, shielding her from the chaos of the city. He could feel her heart pounding, overwhelmed by vendors pushing their goods, racing children, beggars, the stench of bodies and excrement both human and animal. Large pigs roamed the alleyways. Wagons barreled through the roads, heedless of passersby who dodged the wooden wheels and clomping hooves.

"Here's a fine roast for you," a stout man with a greasy bald head and a long leather apron said as he thrust a live chicken toward Joanie. The hen flapped its wings in her face. Gasping, she turned away, hiding against his back. Still holding tightly to her hand, he twisted his other arm behind him, encircling her, his hand pressing her closer.

Thatch and clay one-story homes and shops soon gave way to stone buildings, two and three-stories tall as they neared Tower Gate. With fewer shops and marketers, the pace of the city slowed as did Joanie's heartbeat. Alec gently pulled her alongside him, keeping his arm wrapped possessively around her waist.

"We have almost reached the city limits," he said.

She nodded, resisting the urge to expel her breath in relief. Having spent nearly six months within the same four walls, the noise and commotion of the city jolted her to her core. But they were not free from London yet. Her eyes trained on the armored soldiers guarding the gate. The visors of their helmets were open. She glimpsed their hard eyes and the stern set to their lips as people passed beneath their watchful gaze. One of the guards rested his armored fist on the hilt of his sword. The closer they drew to the gate, the closer she pressed to Alec, unable to tear her eyes away from the guard's iron hand.

"Breathe," he whispered in her ear.

But she couldn't. If there was one thing she had learned in her nineteen years, it was the hurt a man could inflict with his fist.

It was not until the city retreated in the distance that she dared to breathe deep the country air. Having been within the confines of London for years, most of that time spent indoors, the farther they walked the more enraptured with her surroundings she became. Bare limbed trees flanked both sides of the road, their branches stretching like a barren canopy across the white winter sky, making her feel small, but for once not in a bad way. In the distance, rolling hills captured her eye, reminding her of her grandmother's music. Again, she wondered what the Highlands of Scotland looked like — the land so loved by her grandmother. The beauty was almost enough to distract her from the tall, mysterious stranger at her side ... almost.

She glanced up at Alec. He no longer held her hand. He walked beside her, his face unreadable, although she could see his eyes scanning the road, the trees, keeping vigilant note of their surroundings. She thought of his arm encircling her, protecting her during their race through the city. Mary did say she could trust him. Still, he looked so hard. Then she remembered, trust him or not, he was her master, although he did take back the money he paid for her — did he own her or not?

"You didn't pay one-hundred silver marks for me in the end, did you?"

"I did not," he answered, not looking at her. "I stole it back."

Then she remembered how he had said that it wouldn't have been the first time he'd stolen money. "You're a criminal?" she burst out.

He glanced down at her for a moment before looking away. "Only in England?"

Her heart started to pound again. "What are you in Scotland?"

"A secret."

"I do not understand."

She waited for an answer, her heart racing faster. Just then his hand snaked out and he clasped hers, pulling her just behind him, once more shielding her — but from what? The crowded streets of London were far behind them. A moment later, a wagon came into view. Warmth from his hand shot through her. The closer the wagon approached, the more heat poured off him. His hand was steady, strong, and yet it felt like motion, churning waves or gusting winds, like his touch was alive. Power coursed through him, and yet, his expression and stance betrayed none of the feeling and tension she felt. His face remained cold.

When the wagon passed, he released her hand, and the warmth that had held her mesmerized was suddenly gone. She felt lost for a moment. She glanced at him sidelong, wondering what magic he possessed.

"I'm part of a network of rebels fighting for Scottish independence."

Her eyes widened in surprise. She had not expected him to tell her anything so revealing, and she could hardly connect the cold English merchant she had first met in the king's palace with this Scottish thief and rebel.

"I was sent to the king's palace to spy for the cause by Abbot Matthew of Haddington Abbey, which is our destination, in case ye were curious."

He had not glanced at her once while he spoke, and by his tone one might have thought he was discussing the condition of the roads upon which they trod, not causes, rebels, and the secrets of the Church and kings.

"Why are you telling me all this? Aren't you worried I will tell someone?"

Alec stopped then and looked down at her. Joanie's wide brown eyes looked up at him with both curiosity and, of course, the one emotion he had come to expect from her: fear. He reached into his satchel and withdrew a hunk of dried meat. He tore it in half and gave her a piece, intentionally grazing his fingers against her skin, touching her. As before, his mind's eye saw nothing, no flashes of memories, no secrets revealed. He had not even seen the old woman since the very first time he heard her sing. When he touched her, he saw nothing, which perplexed him to no end. What made her different? Regardless of why, she was such a relief to his soul. He wanted to keep on touching her simply because he could.

He backed away and leaned against the tree, sliding to the ground. He took a bite of meat and continued to study her. At length, he looked her square in the eye and said, "Nay, I'm not worried that ye might tell someone."

She shied away from his direct gaze, her eyes darting downward to study her hands. "Because who would I tell, right?" she asked. He felt the sob rise in her throat, although her voice betrayed none of the rush of feeling inside her. "I have no one. I'm alone in this world."

He shook his head. "That's not why." He paused for several moments, watching her as she stood. He knew she did not know what to do: sit, stand, run away. "Besides, ye're not alone, are ye?"

She blushed and dipped her head.

His face was still the same, beautiful and cold, like a statue, but she glimpsed something in his eyes like the barest breath of a smile.

"Let's just say, I can see a person for what they really are," he said. They locked eyes again, his burning straight to her soul.

"What do you see in me?" she whispered, walking closer as if beckoned by the hint of warmth she glimpsed beneath his hardness. Slowly, she knelt beside him. His long black hair hung straight past his chest and gleamed in the sun. His black eyes held hers.

"Fear mostly," he said quietly. "Ye're afraid of most everything around ye. And ye're afraid of me. But I have also felt yer strength." He stopped for a minute, considering her. "Ye've more strength in ye then ye realize, I think. But more than anything, I feel yer goodness. Ye've a kind soul, Joanie."

She considered his words. How did he know what he knew? She was afraid of him, not that his words alleviated her fear. In some ways, they made her more afraid.

"Ye need not fear me, Joanie," he said in a soft voice, which wrapped around her as if he caressed her without even touching her.

His black eyes softened as she stared at him. She felt drawn to him, as if the same heat she had felt when he held her hand coiled around her, pulling her closer to the pulse of life that defied his emotionless facade.

He leaned back and rested his head against the tree and closed his eyes. The breeze picked up and lifted his hair and it danced for a moment in sunshine. His upturned face remained impassive but relaxed. His lips were not pressed into a grim line and she could see their fullness. Looking at him, she felt a pang in her heart. He was so beautiful. Her eyes journeyed from his face to his shoulders. His body was strong, leanly built. His hands were hard, his long fingers sleek and effortlessly elegant like the rest of him.

She leaned forward, wishing to touch his skin, to feel the energy that somehow poured from him like a waterfall crashing into a still pool. Then, as if he had read her mind, his eyes remained closed, but he reached out, grazing his fingers across her palm. His touch lasted only a moment.

"Come," he said. The emotion she had thought she detected in his voice was gone. "We are not far from a village. We need supplies and a room for the night."

Chapter Nineteen

Joanie nervously eyed the outskirts of the village. She had enjoyed the silence of the countryside, surrounded by trees dusted white with snow or bathed in crisp air amid open, rolling hills. She glanced sidelong at Alec who walked beside her but did not touch her. His face still maintained a relaxed countenance, which had made her, in turn, feel less ill at ease in his presence. If he had altered his usual facade to make her less afraid of him, it had worked. When they had first set out, she had been terrified at the prospect of being alone with him and his chilly gaze. Now as she looked at the village looming closer and closer, she wished they could go around it and carry on together, just the two of them.

For the first time that day, the wind picked up. A gust of frigid air cut straight through her cloak. She lowered her head slightly to shield her face but voiced no complaint. Still, Alec whisked his own cloak from his shoulders and wrapped the heavy warmth around her.

"How did you know?" she asked, meeting his uncanny eyes and just as quickly turning away.

"'Tis a cold wind. Your cloak is inadequate. It doesn't take a mind reader to know ye might be cold."

She dared to look back at him, cocking a skeptical brow. His unwavering eyes held hers. He made no further confession. So once again she looked away, unable to hold his powerful gaze. After a short while, she could hear sounds of village life, people shouting to each other, marketers calling out to sell their wares, children laughing. Instead of watching the road and the village unfold, she watched him from the corner of her eyes. Slowly, he began to transform. The relaxed set to his mouth settled once more into a hard, grim line. He became like stone — rigid, polished, and cold — a man no one would wish to approach.

They passed the first croft where an old man sat in a chair, eying them suspiciously. Straightaway, she wanted to shrink from sight. Just then a strong hand clasped hers. Once more, Alec stepped slightly in front of her and pulled her close behind him, ever shielding her.

"I do not like crowds."

"I ken," he said.

"How?" she whispered.

He angled his head to the side so that he could glance down at her. For a moment, his hard facade softened. "I told ye. I can feel ye."

Her brows came together as she considered this. "Do you mean to say you can feel what I feel?"

He nodded before looking forward again. Once more, his stony gaze stared out, his unbreachable wall fully erected.

"Is it only me or can you feel what others feel?"

The heat passing from his body into hers surged like fire for a moment. His shoulders visibly stiffened. "Everyone," he said, his voice flat. "I feel everyone."

She looked around at the villagers curiously. "Tell me what you feel."

"Do you see that man pulling a wagon?"

She peered around his shoulder and saw a man straining to pull an overloaded wagon. "Yes, I see him."

"He is angry."

"I would be angry too," she said, considering the weight of the load he was trying to move on his own.

"Nay, he's not frustrated. He's angry. The kind of anger that drives men to stupid acts."

"What else?" she asked.

"More anger, jealousy, happiness..." He stopped short. She followed his gaze and saw a small boy peering around the side of one of the market stalls. "Fear," Alec said.

"The little boy, you mean?"

He nodded. "Come," he said, and gently pulled her toward the boy.

She held tightly to Alec's hand as they wove through the busy market square to where the boy stood. When he saw their approach, his eyes widened before he turned and ran. Alec released Joanie's hand and overtook the small boy in a just a few strides, grabbing him by the back of his tunic.

"Let me go," the boy shouted.

Joanie watched as Alec shifted his hold from the boy's tunic to his arm. Then Alec squatted in front of him so that they were eye to eye.

"Hush now, lad," Alec said, his voice quiet and gentle. He masked his Scottish brogue once again to sound English. Joanie knew he did this so as not to frighten the boy. "Or whoever you are hiding from is sure to find you."

The boy's eyes widened like big moons ready to swallow his face. "I'm not hiding."

"It is alright." He looked up at Joanie and motioned for her to squat down too. "We're not going to hurt you."

Joanie nodded and smiled a little to try to reassure him. She knew all too well how it felt to be small, surrounded by giants, and utterly afraid. She glanced at Alec and swallowed a gasp. She had never seen his face so warm. He almost looked boyish, as if he and the lad were one and the same.

"What is it?" Alec asked, his voice almost a whisper. "What are you so worried about? I think you came here for help, but you are too afraid to ask."

The boy's eyes darted from Alec to Joanie, then back to Alec.

"My mum is sick," he said, tears pooling in his eyes.

Alec reached out then and placed his hand on the boy's shoulder and closed his eyes. After a moment, his eyes flew open. "Take us to her," he urged the child.

The boy ran away from the village toward distant woods.

Alec grabbed her hand. "Come," he urged. "His mother is in pain. I will explain after we have tried our best to save her."

They followed the small boy deep into the woods. Suddenly, a cry rent the air. Pain gripped Alec. Dropping Joanie's hand, he raced ahead toward a thick copse of oak trees. He could see her and feel her heartbeat. But then another heartbeat filled him, and he realized the boy's mother was about to have a baby. Not wishing to alarm her, he slowed down when he passed through the trees. The moment he locked eyes with the woman, he softened his face, imbued his eyes with warmth and said, "I will not hurt you. You're safe. Your son asked me and my wife to help you, and that is what we are going to do."

Fear pulsed through her, but then another birthing pain came on and she cried out. Alec knelt and took her hand and wrapped his arm around her, supporting her back.

"Breathe," he said, his voice calm and low. The woman gripped his hand. He could feel her body lean into his trustingly. Just then the boy thundered through the trees, a stricken look on his face, with Joanie following just behind him, breathless from running. A moment of confusion flashed across her face, then her eyes widened with recognition. Immediately, she pulled out the ale from her satchel and squatted next to the woman, helping her sip the amber liquid. Then she turned to the boy. "Fetch some water."

Eyes wide, he ran off.

The woman closed her eyes, quiet for a moment, so Alec laid her back on the ground and started to clear away a more comfortable place for her to lie.

"But the boy said she was ill," Joanie whispered as she pulled out one of Alec's tunics from his satchel to swaddle the baby in when it arrived.

"He believes she is. He must not realize that she is having a baby or that pain is a natural part of childbirth."

"I have never assisted a birth, but I am a skilled healer."

"Are ye?" he asked, looking at her curiously.

She met his gaze. "Didn't you know that already?"

He shook his head. "There is little I know of ye."

"How can that be?" she asked. "I'm confused."

He reached for her hand and held it, closing his eyes. Still, he saw nothing. "So am I."

Joanie chewed her lip. "I do not have my herbs. There is little I can do if something goes wrong."

Alec looked at her. "The baby's heart is strong. Both mother and babe will be fine."

An hour later, just as Alec promised, the woman pushed a healthy baby girl into Joanie's awaiting arms. Her son cheered next to her. He had been very relieved when he returned with the water to know that his mother wasn't dying, but that she was having a baby.

Joanie smiled down at the new life in her arms. Then she swaddled her and presented her to her mother. "You have a beautiful baby girl," Joanie said.

She reached for her baby. Tears streaming down her face, she kissed the new infant all over. Then she looked at Alec and Joanie. "Bless you both."

The woman told them her name was Alma and her son was Edgar, named after his father, who'd been flogged to death last winter for starting an uprising against his lord. They were serfs, and Alma had been locked in the stocks for a month. After they released her, she and Edgar had waited until nightfall and ran into the woods. They'd been running ever since.

Joanie set to work washing Alma while Alec laid out some supper of dried meat and bannock.

"Where will you stay the night?" he asked.

"Right here," Alma said. "We are safest in the wood."

"But you cannot light a fire to stay warm or else you risk discovery. Let me get you a room at the inn."

Alma frowned and held her baby tighter. "No. It is too dangerous. You know what will happen if we are caught."

Alec nodded grimly. He placed the last of the food next to her. Then he took his large, warm cloak and spread it out, covering all three.

"If you are able to walk on the morrow, go to the village of Kitwick. It is not three miles east of here."

Alma nodded. "I know the place."

"Go to the Raven's Wing tavern and ask for Henry. Tell him St. Paul sent you. He will help you."

Alma reached for Alec's hand and pressed a kiss to it. "Bless you," she said. "Bless your heart."

Alec dipped his head to Alma and laid his hand on the baby's head. Then he turned to Edgar. "Take care of them, always," he said. Then he stood and outstretched his arm to Joanie.

"Now, I understand," Joanie said as she followed Alec from the woods. "You are a seer. My grandmother told me about people like you. She even claimed to be touched by the Sight herself, although it was her sister who was meant to be truly gifted."

"The sight runs in yer bloodline?" he asked, looking at her curiously, wondering if that could help explain why the stone around his neck remained warm in her presence.

"I suppose it does," Joanie said. Then she canted her head to one side as she studied him. "So, who is Saint Paul?"

Alec raised his brow at her. "Ye caught that, did ye? Well, my brothers and I were first asked to join the cause by the Bishop Lamberton. He called us the Saints and gave us masks and swords. At his command, we robbed English nobles on the road north into Scotland. But during a heist we couldn't use our Christian names. And so, the bishop gave us saints' names. I was Saint Paul. My eldest brother, Jack, was Saint Peter. Quinn, also older than me, was Saint Augustine. Then Rory—"

"Do you mean to say you have more brothers?"

"Two more, and a sister."

She smiled. "I always wished for brothers and sisters. Diana became a sister to me—" her voice broke.

He stopped and turned to face her. "I'm so sorry, Joanie."

She looked up at him. His eyes did not hold the compassion of his voice, but then she realized, they were near the village — he kept them both shielded with his unapproachable facade.

"I, too, know what it is to lose a sister," he said softly. "I used to have two sisters. Rosalyn, the youngest of us all, perished along with my parents when the English invaded Berwick seven years ago. His army destroyed the city, claiming the lives of thousands of Scotsmen and their families, women and children alike."

Joanie gasped, struck by the horror of it all. Now, it was clear to her why he had become a secret Scottish rebel. They continued toward the village in silence, but then Joanie gave Alec a sidelong glance, a question burning in her mind could not wait. "What did you do with the English noble's money?"

He kept his eyes trained forward. "It wasn't their money. It was Scotland's. We were just taking it back. Every coin and bauble went to the cause, rebuilding Scotland's army and feeding those who suffered the wrath of Edward's ambition."

She could hardly believe what she was hearing. Mysterious and seemingly dangerous English Merchant, Randolph Tweed, was, in fact, a Scottish hero.

"It is too late to gather supplies. We will stay the night in the village and set out in the morning."

Joanie turned toward the sun, which dipped low against the horizon, painting the thatch and stone cottages in hues of rose and amber. "Where will we sleep?"

"At the inn."

She tripped on her own feet in her surprise. "Together?"

He caught her arm, keeping her from falling. She heard the amusement in his voice. "Aye, lass," he said. "Together."

Chapter Twenty

He held her hand and walked just slightly in front of her, having felt her heart begin to quicken the moment they entered the center of the village. At that late hour, the streets were not nearly as busy as they had been when the sun still shone overhead; however, some people still milled about, eying Joanie and Alec with suspicion, making her increasingly nervous. He too would have preferred a wooded camp or farm over a bustling village, but only to escape the constant barrage of human emotion that assailed his senses whenever anyone stood near. Clearly, Joanie had the same preference for isolation, but his heart ached, knowing it was her fear of being hurt. Life had taught her that men were cruel and that those more powerful crushed the weaker. She hid for survival. Pulling her closer behind him, he shielded her, wishing he could block out the world around them. But once they had what they needed for the journey north, they could avoid cities and villages until they made it to Haddington Abbey.

"A room for myself and my wife," he told the proprietor of the only inn in the village.

The man scowled at Alec for several moments, his hands resting on his rotund stomach, before he finally outstretched his hand for payment. Alec could feel his instant aversion, but he was unmoved. He was used to people's suspicion. He knew he made himself disagreeable, but what people didn't realize was that Alec was simply keeping them out of his mind. He was careful to avoid touching the man when he dropped the coins into his palm. Judging by his open disdain of Alec, the surly way he eyed Joanie, and the fear in the hearts of the people who worked for him, Alec had no wish to see inside his dark soul. Once the mind had seen something, it could not be unseen, and so many dark images already filled Alec's mind.

"Betty, show them upstairs," the man barked at a young maid carrying a bucket. She jumped a little at the harsh command, causing water to slosh on the floor.

"And watch what you're doing, you lazy cow!"

Fear and fury shot out from Joanie's heart straight into Alec's. He snaked his hand out and grabbed the innkeeper's tunic, pulling him hard against his high table. The moment he touched him, Alec knew he was a thief. Grim images flashed before his eyes, but one came to the fore. The innkeeper finished most evenings at the corner table near the hearth with some shop owners in the village.

Alec leaned close and in a low voice for the innkeeper's ears only, he said, "Be kinder to those around you, or I will tell those who trust you what really happened to their money."

The innkeeper froze, ceasing his struggles. "How did you ...which one of those bastards..." The innkeeper's eyes nigh bulged from his face as he sputtered. A breath later, a nervous smile stretched his lips wide. Casting his gaze sidelong at the maid, he said, "No worries, Betty dear. I will just have Robert clean—"

Alec tightened his grip.

"I ... what I meant to say is that I will clean that up. You just go ahead and take our guests up to their room."

"I have many friends in town," Alec whispered. "I will know if you mistreat anyone again."

Joanie suppressed a smile as she watched Alec slowly release the innkeeper's tunic, but inside she was nigh bursting with pride. She knew naught what he had said to make the man suddenly so obliging, but she was overjoyed to have witnessed him being put in his place. And by the way Betty smiled at Alec, Joanie knew he was not just Scotland's hero anymore.

She followed Betty across the busy common room to the stairs. When they reached the top and started down a long hallway, Betty suddenly whirled around, her face beaming, the blond curls that framed her face danced as she dipped into a low curtsy.

"Thank you," she said, her eyes darting between Joanie and Alec. "I don't know what you said, but I've never seen the master so flustered. He squirmed like the snake he is."

Joanie smiled and glanced at Alec who dipped his head to acknowledge the young maid's praise but kept silent.

Betty did not seem to mind, however, as she turned and prattled on about telling her mother when she left for the evening. "Supper is served in an hour downstairs," she said, opening the door to their room.

"Would you mind bringing us a tray when time allows?" Alec asked.

She bobbed in a curtsy, her smile still beaming. "It would be my pleasure."

Alec simply nodded and motioned for Joanie to enter.

"Goodnight," she said to Betty.

A moment later, Alec shut the door behind him and leaned against the slatted wood for a moment. She watched him close his eyes and take several steadying breaths.

"Is it quiet now ... inside of you, I mean?"

He shook his head. "Nay, I feel them everywhere, but 'tis as if it's muffled now. Like a dream or even a ghostly presence."

"Like you're haunted."

Alec locked eyes with her. "Exactly."

Joanie felt her heart pound as she met Alec's gaze. His black eyes were always intense — either cold and hard like an iron wall, almost hurtful in how they blocked out life, or they were probing, searching as if he were deep inside her.

At that moment, she was acutely aware of him, not just his intensity, but she was aware of him as a man. He stood straight and walked toward her. He seemed to fill the room with his height and powerful presence. She did not feel unsafe. On the contrary, she believed him when he said he would never hurt her. Still, she was painfully nervous. She didn't know what to do or say.

When he stopped in front of her, she craned back her neck to meet his gaze. "We're alone," she suddenly blurted.

Embarrassed, she turned away and started to wander the room, touching the faded blue covering on the platform bed and grazing her fingertips across the table that was positioned in front of the shuttered window. From the corner of her eye, she watched him cross the room to the cold hearth. He moved with quiet ease. He was such a tempting combination of effortless elegance and confident ability. He squatted down and began to light a fire. She could not help but admire the way his back tapered to his narrow waist and the strong lines of his thigh and curve of his buttock.

"Oh God," she said under her breath before she turned away.

Diana had often spoken of men with admiration for their bodies. She would occasionally reminisce about past lovers and tease Joanie for turning a bright shade of crimson whenever she did. Joanie never truly believed her when she said that some men could be gentle with a woman and make a woman's body soar with pleasure. But now, having witnessed Alec's quiet confidence, his powerful strength, and his undeniable kindness, she could not help but wonder if there was any truth to Diana's stories.

"Ye're not afraid of me anymore," he said quietly.

She jumped, startled by his voice. She turned around. He stood now, tall and lean, with his back still to her.

Did he know the true direction of her thoughts? Panicked, she searched the room for some way to hide from him. But he turned then and looked at her. "Now what are ye afraid of?"

She froze mid-step — to where she did not know. There was no escaping him, and even if she could, she knew escape was not what she really wanted.

"You again," she said. Then she looked down at her feet. "And my own thoughts," she said truthfully.

He did not answer, and so she forced herself to once more meet his gaze. The hardness had once more fled his face, but his gaze was no less probing, no less intense.

"Sit with me."

She clasped her hands in front of her, and then she crossed her arms over her chest. "You mean, you want me to come over there?" she asked, wishing to keep a room between them.

She felt this pit of longing in her stomach, like hunger but for something she had never imagined before. It was as if her very soul was starved, but then memories of the abuse and ha-

tred that had been her life's story flashed before her eyes —
what was she thinking? Her soul had never been fed before.

"Don't be sad," he whispered, suddenly standing in front of
her. She looked up and lost herself in his eyes. They were soft
with concern. "So sad," he said, his voice barely above a whisper as he reached out his hand. He hesitated, his fingers nearly grazing her cheek. But then he touched her, so softly at first.
She closed her eyes as the now familiar warmth shot through
her. She felt the pulsing life that filled his soul touch her very
heart, her own soul. He stepped even closer. She was surrounded by the heat of him, the feel of him, the scent of him, and
everything within her wanted more. He cupped her cheeks between his hands and brought his forehead to hers.

"Ye're magic," he whispered.

A burst of laughter rushed from her lips. She stared up at
him with incredulity but then succumbed to the lulling motion
of his touch. She closed her eyes to savor the feeling before saying, "Of the two of us, I'm sure you are the one with magic."

He stepped away suddenly. She opened her eyes, shocked
by the swift retraction of his touch. "Ye don't understand," he
said, his arms stiff at his sides, his hands tightly fisted. "I do not
touch people," he said, his black eyes boiling with emotion. "At
least not willingly."

He flexed his fingers and looked down at his hands. "When
I touch someone, I step inside them. I see their sins, their fears,
their pain. I see the faces of people they have loved, or hurt, or
lost."

He raked both his hands through his long hair. The moment before he spun away from her, she saw such an ache of
suffering in his eyes, it brought tears to her own. She stared

now at his back, knowing he fought to regain the control he worked so hard to constantly maintain. When he turned back around, his impassive mask shaped the contours of his face. Her beautiful statue stood in front of her, but now she did not fear him. Now she understood.

Slowly, the hardness left his eyes, and he again stepped toward her. She held her breath as he drew closer still. Then he reached out his hand, and just his fingertips grazed hers. His touch ignited her soul, compelling her to weave her fingers together with his.

"When I touch ye," he breathed, "I see nothing but ye. I am just a man. Ye're just a woman." A shiver shot from his body into hers, and she could not help but think that he was far from just a man. She looked up and met his gaze.

He swallowed hard. "I cannot tell ye how good it feels," he said, his voice low. He drew her cloak away and reached for the last few pins sloppily containing her hair. "So beautiful," he whispered.

She bent her head, unable to bear his kindness, his gentleness. Tears stung her eyes. Longing filled her with his every breath caressing her cheek. Warm and so close, it hurt as much as it pleased.

"Still so sad," he said, crooking her chin and gently lifting her head so that he could see her face. "I cannot see yer truth. Ye must tell me."

She swallowed the knot in her throat. "What do you want to know?"

"Ye," he implored. "I want to know ye."

Flashes of fists, knives, whips, and pokers combined with hurtful words — she did not want him to know her truth. It was too ugly.

"I know that emotion all too well," he said, his voice soothing. "Ye've been hurt, Joanie. A lifetime of hurt. But the shame is not yers. None of it is yers. Do ye hear me?"

His searching eyes and full lips blurred like a dream as tears welled over her lids. "The scars across my body will tell you the story of who I am, how I came to be ... me."

Once more he cupped her cheeks, and he lowered his head and gently kissed away a tear from her cheek, then another. Holding her gaze, he let his hands fall to his sides. "Let me see ye as ye really are."

She couldn't bear the idea of Alec seeing the ugliness that marred her body. Although healed over on the outside, each wound cut soul-deep. Inside, she still bled. How could she let him see?

"Do not be afraid. Trust in me," he whispered.

Her breath caught. Dare she? Dare she truly trust Alec with her life, her story. She found her courage. "I do this for me," she said quietly.

Hands trembling, she reached for her tunic and pulled it slowly over her head. The warmth of the fire caressed her shoulders. Her heart pounded, but she refused to turn back. Drawing a deep breath, she lifted the hem of her kirtle and eased her tattered hose from her hips, peeling them down each leg.

Then she stood before him, head down and eyes closed, clad in naught but her sheer kirtle.

Pressing her lips together, she fought the desire to scream, to sob — for she knew what he saw — the layers of red lashes that covered her back and stomach. The burn marks. The angry bruises still marring her skin from her last fight with Geoffrey.

She opened her eyes when she felt his hands gently circle her waist. She gasped at the sight of his black eyes burning with midnight fire. Furious waves of heat emanated from his hands that held her so gently but burned her soul with the fire raging within him.

"Who did this?" he growled, the very words seemed to pain him. "Who hurt ye?"

A sob tore from her throat. "My father." She drew a shaky breath. "And every master who has owned me since."

He ran a thumb along the scar across her collarbone that slashed her chest.

"That was a knife," she whispered. "It was the closest I ever came to dying."

He bent down and kissed where he had touched. The heat from his lips soothed below the surface, penetrating beyond layers of skin to where the true scars resided. She reached her arms around his neck, weaving her hands through his hair and closed her eyes. His lips trailed down her chest and stomach, kissing every hurt through the thin fabric of her kirtle. He turned her around, his hands and lips spreading his magic breath and heat over her, inside her, everywhere. Then he circled around her and stood in front of her, his black eyes now glistening with her story. She expelled a breath she felt she had been holding her whole life as he lifted her into his arms. Cradling her, he crossed to the bed. Lying beside her, he held her in his arms. She closed her eyes, feeling his strength surround her.

"Never again," he whispered over and over until at last she believed him.

Chapter Twenty One

Joanie slowly stretched, savoring the warmth and restfulness that filled her limbs. She had never slept better. It had been a night without fear that someone might come through the door with fist raised or tongue ready to sting. She opened her eyes and saw Alec sitting in front of the open window, his feet crossed and resting on the ledge while he crunched down on an apple.

"Good morrow," he said without looking at her. She realized as she swung her legs over the edge of the bed that he saw her even though his eyes gazed out beyond the ledge. He knew she had risen because he would have felt her awaken. He saw in ways others could not.

"Good morrow," she answered, reaching her arms heavenward. He turned then and met her gaze. Somehow, he looked different, warmer, like a patch of earth that had thawed in the sunshine. She realized he was younger than she had thought. He could not have been older than five and twenty. He held his body with such ease that she could not help but smile. And then something happened that made her gasp, her heart nigh full to bursting. The corners of his lips rose like the sun, and a smile spread across his face, making her knees weak. She did not trust herself to stand.

"Come," he said, still smiling. "Break your fast, for we've much to accomplish before we set out. I wish to be on the road before noon."

Blushing, she glanced down at her lap while she waited for her heart to stop racing. After a few moments, she dared to look up. Smiling, too, she accepted his hand and sat next to him by the window.

"Where did this come from?" she said, accepting the rosy apple he offered.

"Last night, Betty left a tray outside our door," he said, pointing to the table.

She glimpsed rolls and cheese. Her stomach growled at the sight. Bringing the apple to her lips, she took a big bite. While she chewed, she peered out the window at the street below and breathed in the crisp morning air. From above, she enjoyed the sight of children playing and people milling with purposeful strides over the frost-covered road.

Feeling a slight pressure on her shoulder, she looked up at Alec who now stood behind her, gently pushing her shoulders away from her ears.

"Yer body needs to learn to not always be guarding itself." With his hands on her shoulders, she felt tall. She straightened her spine and grew longer, but when he removed his hands, her shoulders instinctively shot up around her ears.

"We'll work on that," he said, his lips upturned.

She looked up at him, mesmerized by the warmth in his eyes. Slowly, he lowered his head, bringing his lips a breath away from hers. Her stomach fluttered. Her heart pounded. And then he closed his eyes and kissed her. She trembled beneath his gentle touch. The apple rolled from her hand forgotten to the floor as she closed her eyes and felt the heat of his touch pulse through her. Then she stood and wrapped her arms around his neck. He deepened their kiss, and she pressed into him. All his fire whirled around her like a blazing windstorm making her heart race faster. He filled her empty soul with longing and an ache so sweet it curled her toes and made her knees weak.

When he slowly pulled away, she felt somehow like they were still connected, still touching. She'd been branded by his kiss, forever changed by her first taste of passion.

His eyes bore into hers with an intensity like never before, but his words were gentle, setting her racing heart as ease. "After tasting yer lips, I cannot imagine being sated by mere bread and cheese, but we should probably finish our meal."

She nodded incapable of containing her smile.

After they finished eating, she put on her cloak.

"Are ye ready?" he asked gently.

She took a deep breath, wishing they could remain in that room for the rest of the day, the rest of their lives.

He grabbed the latch on the door and held it open for her. After closing the door behind him, he clasped her hand and stepped slightly in front of her, keeping her just behind him. She watched the warmth flee his face, replaced once more by his stony mask. Behind his impenetrable wall of cold indifference, she happily hid from the world as they made their way from the inn.

Marketers had set up on the village green. Moving from stall to stall, he bought her new leather slippers and a cloak of thick worsted wool. He also bought a new cloak for himself to replace the one he had given Alma. For their journey, he filled a satchel with dried meat and several fresh bannock, and lastly, they stopped at the stables where he paid forty crowns for a chestnut-colored horse.

As planned, they left the village just as the sun rose above their heads. On the outskirts of town, he brought the horse around and began arranging their supplies in saddlebags. She eyed the large beast nervously. She had never sat a horse before. Chewing her lip, she readied her courage to mount. But Alec looked at her with his seeing eyes and offered her his hand. Pulling the horse behind him, they set out on foot while sunlight glistened on the frost still clinging to the bracken. Her breath hung in front of her, but she did not feel cold walking beside Alec. With his hand clasped tightly in her own, he warmed her from the inside out, and about her shoulders hung the most wondrous cloak.

"You are even more beautiful when you smile," he said softly, looking down at her from his great height.

She blushed, her hands rushing to her cheek. "I didn't realize I was smiling."

"Don't stop," he said, cupping her cheek. He slowly lowered his lips to hers, and she softened in his arms. His full lips molded to hers, filling her with warmth. His touch was gentle and yet so deeply felt. When he pulled away, she gripped his tunic to keep from falling, her knees trembling from his touch.

"I can't believe ye're real," he said. And the truth of his words shone in his eyes. "Come," he said. "There is someone I want ye to meet."

Drawing her shoulders around her ears, her eyes darted around them, afraid of who might suddenly appear from behind the trees or rise up from the thicket.

"This is Rosie," he said, bringing the horse closer to her.

Realizing there wasn't a stranger hiding nearby, her shoulders eased down a little. "It's a girl?" she asked, looking at the large animal with wide eyes.

"Aye, lass, and named Rosie by the stable master's daughter, like my sister, Rose, which I judged as a good omen. She has a sweet temperament, a strong back, and her hooves are better at negotiating the rocky highlands than yer small feet, even with new slippers. And ... well ... to be honest, Joanie, 'tis in our best interest to reach the border as quickly as we can."

Joanie eyed the mare's great height and muscular body. She did appreciate a good omen.

"I won't let anything happen to ye," Alec promised. "Trust me."

She swallowed and met his gaze. "I trust you," she breathed. Stepping closer to the horse, she straightened her spine and spread her feet apart. "What do I do?" she asked, her voice strong.

Before she could draw her next breath, she was soaring through the air and set astride Rosie's back. In a flash, Alec settled in behind her, pulling her close.

She laughed. "Well, that was simple enough." Then she nuzzled against him, enjoying the feel of his body surrounding hers.

After riding for several hours, he stopped where the road intercepted a river and climbed down before he reached for Joanie. She slid into his arms. "Ye might find yer legs feel a bit weak."

She blushed. "My backside is sore. That much I know already."

"See if ye can stand?"

He placed her on her feet and slowly let go of his hold. Her legs felt like they didn't belong to her, and it pained her when she walked. But the pain was not so great that she couldn't deal with it. Pain was something she had learned to tolerate.

Lifting her chin, she said, "I'm fine."

Alec considered her for a moment, admiring her strength. Then he handed her a costrel. "Have some ale and a bannock. I'm going to take Rosie down to the river."

Rushing currents wound among large rocks that jutted from beneath the restless surface of the river, ever changing, ever moving. The river's song rose out from the earth, expanding the reach of the river to the air, the very clouds. It surrounded him, penetrating his heart and mind, a welcome change from the harsh, abrasive sounds of the city. While Rosie dropped her muzzle to the undulating currents, he stared back at Joanie. She nibbled on a piece of bannock while she stood, her back long and straight, gazing up at the myriad branches set against the cool sky. They fanned out in wild disarray, bare and starved for warmth. She was like those branches. The harshness of life had stripped her down to a shell, exposed, unadorned, but just beneath the surface teemed ferocious vitality. How he admired her strength. He knew the ride must have left her aching, and yet she made no complaint. She pushed on. She would survive. That is what she'd spent a lifetime doing, surviving one unthinkable horror after another. He fought the rush of fury that blazed within him when he thought of the scars that crisscrossed her bare limbs. But in time, if she came to know the security of roots planted firmly in the warm earth, then she too could grow and stretch, and become the woman so many had tried to cut down.

He pressed his hand to his chest, feeling the secret shard. The abbot had said that the fate of Scotland resided in the mystery of the stone — but how could Joanie be tied to Scotland's fate? He worried for her, wanting to protect her from ever knowing harm again. A sudden flurry of emotions blasted his heart, turning his thoughts from Joanie. He closed his eyes, absorbing the faint but unmistakable nearness of other souls. Men approached, their minds disciplined and purposeful.

He pulled on Rosie's reigns. "Come to me," he said to Joanie. He took the costrel from her hand and shoved it in one of the bags. Then he clasped her waist and lifted her onto Rosie's back. Swinging up behind her, he drove his heels into the horse's flanks and galloped off toward the woods.

A jolt of fear shot through Joanie. Alec had turned to steel before her eyes. "What happened?" she gasped once they were beneath the sparse canopy provided by the bare trees.

"A large band of warriors, English soldiers most likely, was moving quickly toward us on the road."

"How did you...?" Her question trailed off unfinished from her lips. She already knew the answer. He had felt them coming.

"We'll stay off the roads from here on out. It will take us longer to reach the border, but it will be safer."

"I rather prefer it in here than on the open road," she said, nestling deeper into his arms. She felt enclosed, protected from every direction. His strong arms encircled her, and the trees surrounded them both. Overhead, the branches wove an intricate canopy, delicate but strong, like fine lace on a burlap backing. The weave permitted streaks of light to pass inside and touch her cheeks but guarded against all other intruders — or so she allowed herself to believe. She loved everything about that moment — the strength of Alec's long and leanly muscled torso against her back, the breath of the forest slowly warming as Spring began to awaken and stretch, still hidden but only just beneath the surface. His arms tightened around her, and she sighed, savoring the warmth of his body.

IT WASN'T UNTIL THE last golden light vanished into shadow that Alec eased Rosie to a halt and swung down to the hard earth.

"We will rest here for the night." He laid his cloak on the forest ground, and produced two apples, dried cuts of meat, and two pigeon pies from one of the saddlebags. Then he reached for her, his hands surrounding her small waist, and once more his heart broke at the ubiquity of her suffering. "I intend to fatten ye up, so eat yer fill." He smiled softly. "Just as soon as I drink mine." He kissed her, slowly, gently, like one might sip the very nectar of life itself — something to be savored and cherished.

He pulled away, his harsh breaths contrasting with the gentleness of his touch. "Eat, so I can hold ye without worrying I might break ye."

Joanie's stomach growled as she knelt on his cloak and reached for a pigeon pie. Flakes of buttery crust crumbled on her tunic as she ate. When she was finished, she pinched the crumbs, not letting a speck of the delicious pie go to waste.

"The other one is also for ye," Alec said.

She looked at him, sitting just across from her. He held an apple, which he absently tossed from one hand to another. "You must have more than just an apple," she said.

His smile reached his eyes, which shone at her like black suns, bright and hot. He shrugged. "I will have some meat and bannock as well. Anyway, I am particularly fond of apples. My wee sister, Rosalyn, and my mother used to sell them on market days."

"You still grieve for them," Joanie said, knowingly.

"I always will. Once grief enters someone's soul it is there forever. It has a different feeling than sadness or fear, although both are present in grief. When it is fresh, it screams. It's raw and impossible to contain. But after a while, it disappears from the surface, sinking deep like a river that runs through ye. It becomes part of ye, always present but quiet, like the low notes in a song." He reached for her hand. "Ye seem warm enough," he said before crunching into his apple. "I dare not risk lighting a fire."

She smiled, folding her cloak tighter around herself. "I've never felt so warm." And that was true. Never had she owned such a fine cloak, but more than that, Alec always gave off a wave of heat that kept her warm to her core. He was her own living, breathing flame. She took a bite of her second pie and took in the sight of him. Her eyes traveled down the white skin of his neck to the V of his tunic where she glimpsed sleek muscles. She wondered what his skin would feel like to touch. Then she noticed the thick twine around his neck.

"Do you wear something around your neck?"

He lowered his eyes as the warmth in his face fled. He didn't turn hard or cold, just emotionless.

"I'm sorry," she said. "I didn't mean to pry."

"Nay, it is not that. 'Tis just that, I'm not quite certain what it is myself." She watched as he reached into his shirt and took out the shard of stone.

"Oh," she said. "So that is the hardness I have felt."

He held the stone up to his black eyes. "Have ye also felt its warmth?"

She smiled. "You always feel warm to me."

He continued to study the stone. "Abbot Matthew gave it to me. It is a mystery to him as well. Although he knows more than he was willing to share, he did say it was important to our cause. His hope is that I will see whatever secrets the stone keeps. But so far, I have not been able to see anything. Well ... that is until ye came along."

"Me? Whatever do you mean?"

He took the stone from his neck and held it out to her. "Feel," he said.

She touched her fingers to the stone, then pulled quickly away. "It is warm," she said, surprised, having expected it to be cold like any normal stone would be.

"It wasn't always like this," he said. "It only grows warm when ye are near me or in my thoughts. Ye heat the stone."

Her eyes grew wide. "How could I make that happen?"

Alec smiled at her. "Should it be so hard to believe that ye're special, Joanie? Ye have infinite strength inside of ye. 'Tis how ye survived this long. Ye have the healing touch. I felt how ye soothed Alma." He cupped her cheek. "And somehow, ye quiet the thunder of voices within me."

"I do?" She wasn't exactly sure what he meant, but, after all he had done to help her, the idea that she somehow made his life better filled her with the greatest joy she had ever known.

"Ye do. And every day I notice it more. Yer presence does not silence the voices, nor does it block the emotions from entering my mind and heart, but ye soften the blow, taking away some of the sting. Ye have yer own gift, which I believe ye inherited from yer grandmother."

Joanie considered this. "My grandmother was special. She was a great healer and taught me everything she could. She would wake me up after my father had fallen into a drunken sleep, and together we would grind herbs and mix remedies." Joanie missed her so much.

"When did she die?" he asked softly.

She looked beyond where he sat to the sky, silvery and purple in the twilight. "She died when I was very young."

"She was Scottish, wasn't she?"

She cocked a brow at him. "How could you feel that she was Scottish?"

He laughed, and the sound struck her heart, bringing a smile to her own lips.

"I guessed that time. I remembered the songs ye sang at the palace, songs about the old ways. Ye had to learn them from someone. How old were ye when she died?"

Her smile vanished and a knot formed in her throat. "I was eight years old. I didn't even get a chance to say goodbye to her."

"What happened?"

"She had been ill for several days. I tried to stay by her side, to treat her and soothe her, but my father refused me. I had to go to the tavern where I worked washing the floors every morning. But the tavern keeper kept me there until late in the night, cleaning tankards. When I returned home, she had died." She swallowed hard. "He had already buried her there, in unhallowed ground, without ceremony or even a marker. I fashioned a cross myself that night. But he dug it up and used it to light the morning fire. He sold me one week later."

Alec reached for her and pulled her into his arms. "If I could take it all away, I would," he said.

"I don't need the old to go away. I just need the new to be better," she said softly.

"Is this better?" He cupped her face and kissed her with soft insistence.

"So much better," she murmured, wrapping her arms around his neck.

Alec laid down and wrapped his body around her from behind, spooning her. He breathed the scent of her and noticed how her shoulders still hugged her ears. He slid his hand onto the top of her shoulder and pushed down. When he moved his hand away, it popped back up. Again, he pressed down on her shoulder. "Relax," he crooned in her ear. "Ye're fine. Ye're safe and warm. I will never let anyone hurt ye again. Ever." Once more it popped back up when he removed his hand. He smiled when he heard her chuckle.

"Are ye doing that on purpose?"

"I swear I'm not." She twisted her neck to look back at him. "I know I seem tense, but I'm truly not. I've never felt so at ease." Then she snuggled into his body, her shoulders hugging her ears. "This feels good to me."

He wrapped his arms around her, pulling her tightly against him. "Nothing has ever felt so good."

Chapter Twenty Two

Alec and Joanie struck camp early every morning and rode until the last light faded. With a canopy of stars and bare interwoven branches overhead, they would fall asleep in each other's arms, their souls clutching the promise glimpsed in the other's eyes.

On the seventh morning, Joanie sat near the fire while Alec readied their horse. A fae wind cut through the wood, stirring the faded, shriveled leaves at her feet. They twisted around her before the wind carried them off through the woods. The frosty breeze had left her heart cold. Her eyes darted around her, her chest suddenly feeling tight. Sinking beneath a wave of apprehension, she buried her head within the protective strength of her shoulders. Shallow breaths filtered in and out of her mouth, barely feeding her lungs — and then she paused.

The wind had died down. Soft morning light slanted through the tall trees. She gazed up at the clear blue sky. The rich cerulean hue carried the promise of Spring. Forcing herself to take a slow, deep breath, she eased her shoulders back in place. Still, she had to work to let her guard down.

She closed her eyes and breathed even deeper, life giving breaths. Stretching her neck to the left, then the right, she allowed her legs to uncurl from her chest and spread out in front of her. Then she leaned back on her hands and lifted her face to the sky. After several minutes, Alec appeared in her line of vision. He looked down at her with warmth in his deep-set eyes, a gentle smile curving his lips.

"Ye're humming," he said.

Her eyes widened for a moment, and then she smiled. "I was, wasn't I?"

He squatted down next to her and pressed his hand to her heart. She closed her eyes and savored his heat and the surge of wellbeing that coursed through her.

"In time, yer body will know this is as it should be."

His words made her heart swell. "Promise?" she whispered, lost in the affection she found in his gaze.

When he smiled, it changed his whole face. His eyes shone. It was as if everything that she felt when she touched him — the rhythmic pulse of power deep within him — had suddenly broken free, and it made him shine. And for a moment, he was light. A shining light setting her dark world aflame.

He held out his hand. "I've good tidings."

She allowed him to pull her to her feet.

"We will be in Scotland before the sun sets."

In another time, with someone different at her side, she might have been terrified by the prospect of heading farther north into wild, unfamiliar lands. But not now. Not with Alec. Hope surged through her. Her beloved grandmother had hailed from Scotland. The music that had kept her soul strong first traveled from the lips of those who had made their homes among the heather, the melodies reaching her ears on the currents of Highland winds. She had always dreamed of seeing those rugged, distant mountains and rolling moors with her own eyes, and now, on this very day she would be in Scotland.

"Come," she said, grabbing Alec's hand and pulling him toward Rosie.

His deep, quiet laughter followed her. "To think only days ago, I had to convince ye to give Rosie a chance."

She stopped and turned to face him. "Who would have believed that one life could be so altered in such a short time?"

He gently pulled her against him and cupped her cheeks. "Two lives," he said, softly correcting her. Then he bent his head low and brushed his lips against hers, a whispered caress that made her ache for more. Then he deepened his kiss, his full lips claiming hers. She threw her arms around his neck and returned his kiss with all her passion, all her strength.

Still not breaking their connection, he scooped her into his arms, cradling her as he crossed to the mare. Only when he lifted her onto Rosie's back did their lips part. She knew the heat she saw in his gaze, mirrored her own desire. He slid into the saddle behind her.

"Mayhap we stay here one more day," she breathed, her hand stroking his strong thigh. His arms came around her, and he kissed her again with feverish passion. Her heart pounded. A sweet ache ignited like wildfire deep within her. She never knew that some pain could feel so good.

Alec tore his lips from hers. "I want nothing more than to lay ye down within that alcove of birch trees and love every inch of ye, body and soul." But then the familiar darkness deepened the color of his eyes, and the beautiful lines of his face hardened. "But not here. Not on this land. We ride for Scotland."

Several hours later, just as the sun dipped below the horizon and the world was painted a vibrant pink, their mount cleared the edge of a thick wood. Before her, rolling moors stretched out like a faded, frosty sea.

"*Alba gu bràth*," he whispered in her ear. "Scotland forever."

"Scotland forever," she repeated, tears filling her eyes when she realized she had truly made it. For so long, her heart had traveled north to this place to escape the pain of the moment, and she had dreamed that one day, she could leave it all behind. At long last, the nightmare had ended, and her dreams were finally coming true.

Chapter Twenty Three

They rode on for another hour through a patch of dense woods. Then once more, Rosie nosed through two Scot pines and stepped onto a field. Stubby remains of oat stalks from the last harvest dotted the large swath of land, and on the opposite side, Joanie spied a long thatch and clay hut. Smoke coiled out from the rooftop toward the darkening sky. Straightaway, a wave of apprehension shot through her.

Alec wrapped his arm tighter around her. "Ye've not to fear. This is the home of Hamish and Helena Dunaid. They are allies to the cause, and friends to the MacVie family."

Joanie closed her eyes, willing away her fear. "Why are we here?"

"We are going to call on them for a visit."

Alec had never made a social call in his life. In fact, if any of his brothers knew he was going to visit the Dunaid croft, they'd likely draw a sword on him and demand to know who he was and what he had done with their brother. He glanced up at the sky. Writhing clouds, dark and sinister, gathered overhead, quickly consuming the few stars shining in the twilight sky. A storm was building, and he did not want Joanie to suffer through a sleepless night of pelting rain and booming thunder.

More than that, there was another reason that compelled him toward the Dunaid croft. Joanie had awakened something within him he had long since thought dead. The Berwick massacre had left him with only a trace of soul. Certainly, he had always been reserved, choosing to remain on the periphery, but his love for his friends and family had mattered to him. Still, after witnessing the brutal and merciless death of so many thousands, he had withdrawn inside himself; his scars running too deep to heal, or so he once thought. Watching Joanie emerge from the shadows of her past had reminded him of how blessed he truly was. He had been born into a loving family; whereas, Joanie had been delivered into the grip of one monster after another. But tonight, for the first time, she would have a taste of what a real home felt like.

As they rode up to the cottage, Alec spied Hamish rounding up a few chickens. He stopped and waved when he saw their approach.

"Alec MacVie, is that really ye?" he asked, his kind eyes wide with surprise. A gust of wind lifted Hamish's hair and caused Joanie to curl her back into Alec. He swept his cloak in front of her to shield her face from the wind. When he pulled Rosie alongside Hamish, he dismounted and reached for Joanie, setting her feet gently on the ground. He smiled at her encouragingly before he wrapped his arm around her waist and turned to Hamish, who extended his hand to Alec. Alec faltered. He looked at Hamish's hand but did not take it.

Hamish shifted his feet and rubbed the back of his neck instead. "Och, sorry, Alec, I forgot yer odd ways."

Gripping Joanie's waist tighter, Alec took a steadying breath and extended his hand. A slow smile spread across Hamish's face the instant before he clasped Alec's hand. Flashes of Hamish's life came to the fore of Alec's mind—Helena standing in front of him in a crown of wildflowers as they spoke their vows, the birth of their first son, the death of their second—but the images, sounds, and feelings were stifled and hazy, like a dream. He pulled his amazing, healing Joanie even closer and said, "Hamish, I would like ye to meet Joanie Picard. We're heading north to Haddington Abbey and could use a dry spot to rest for the night."

Hamish dipped his head to Joanie, then patted Alec on the back. "Won't Helena be surprised to see ye." Then he winked at Joanie. "And I dare say she'll be undone to have the company of a young lass like yerself."

Hamish opened the door to the cottage, releasing the scent of warm bannock and herbs, and ushered them and the chickens inside. Alec smiled a little when Helena looked up and froze with a large wooden spoon close to her lips. He dipped his head in greeting.

Helena's plump, rosy face blanched. "Sweet Mary and all the Saints," she burst out. "Alec MacVie, is that really ye standing there, smiling at me, or are ye some kind of specter come to haunt my home?"

Alec's slight smile widened, and Helena stumbled back a little, making the sign of the cross. "Hamish!"

Hamish crossed the room and wrapped his arm around her. "Calm yerself. 'Tis only Alec. He's asked to wait out the rain here with us."

Alec stepped forward. "If it's not too much trouble."

A slow smile spread across Helena's face. "Aye ... I mean nay ... I mean 'tis no trouble, none at all. I'm delighted ye're here. Shocked, I don't mind telling ye, but delighted." Then her gaze shifted from Alec to Joanie.

Helena walked right over and took her hand. "And who might ye be, lass?" she asked, sweeping Joanie toward the center of the room to the table. Alec pressed his lips together to keep from smiling at the sight of Joanie, small and thin with her shoulders up around her ears and her arms pinned to her sides beneath Helena's broad arm.

"Joanie," she said quietly, her eyes wide.

"Well, ye just sit right down here, Joanie, and I'll pour ye a cup of hot mead. Ye must be chilled to the bone."

"Alec," Hamish said, drawing his gaze away from Joanie sitting stiffly in the chair, uttering one-word responses to Helena who peppered her with questions.

"There's still two goats out on the other side of the field. Will ye give me a hand getting them inside?"

Alec nodded. Then he turned to Joanie. He could feel the rapid pace of her heart. He walked to her side and bent to press a kiss to her cheek. "Ye're safe here," he breathed. Then he straightened. "I'll be right back. I'm just going to give Hamish a hand outside."

Joanie watched Alec follow Hamish out the door. Then she turned back to Helena whose face looked like it could crack she was smiling so hard.

"So that explains it," Helena said, raising her brows.

Joanie shifted uncomfortably in her seat. "What has been explained?"

Helena chortled, giving Joanie a knowing look. Blushing, Joanie grasped her mug with both hands and took a sip but left the mug near her face as her own shield to Helena's probing eyes.

"Alec MacVie has visited my home of his own accord with the closest thing to a smile I have ever seen on his face. And now, I know who put it there," she said, winking at Joanie.

Her cheeks warmed again. She lifted the mug a little higher to hide her rosy hue.

"Don't fash yerself, lass. I can see I'm making ye nervous. Now, why don't ye give me a hand with the soup?"

Relieved to have something to occupy her hands, Joanie hopped to her feet, kept her head downcast and started chopping carrots. Meanwhile, Helena hummed a quiet song. Joanie looked sidelong at the kind woman. She knew Helena was giving her a little space to find her ease. And after several question-free minutes passed, Joanie found herself beginning to relax.

"Be a dear and grab that basket," Helena said, waving her spoon at the wall. "'Tis for the bannock."

Joanie darted across the room and seized the basket.

"Now, if ye don't mind, ye can just pile them in and set it on the table."

Joanie nodded and hastily started to fill the basket, but then Helena touched her hand. Joanie looked up and met her kind eyes. "Hush yer soul, lass. Ye're as tense as the air outside. Ye're safe here with me."

Joanie stopped and lowered her eyes, expelling a slow breath. Then she looked up at Helena. "Thank you," she whispered and began to stack the oatcakes at an easy pace.

After several moments passed, Helena said in a breezy voice, "'Tis nearly seven years now that I've known the MacVie brothers."

Joanie glanced up from the table. She chewed her lip, waiting for Helena to say more. But Helena had renewed her humming while she gave her attention to the pottage she stirred.

Finally, curiosity got the better of her, and at length Joanie asked softly, "How did ye meet them?"

Helena smiled. "My son, Luke, brought them home one summer's eve. Luke is one of the..." she paused, her eyes darting to Joanie, then she looked down at the pot. "They met at church," she said quickly.

Joanie pressed her lips together to suppress a smile. She knew Helena was going to say that Luke was one of Scotland's secret rebels but had changed her mind, not knowing whether Joanie knew about the cause. Joanie held her tongue, deciding Helena was right to be cautious. It was better not to delve too deep into what was secret.

"Anyway," Helena continued, "one night Luke brought them all over to meet us — all five MacVie brothers and the eldest MacVie, their sister, Rose. Good lads, every one of them and so handsome. Jack is the eldest and what a swagger he has. Were I not old enough to be his mother, I might have dreamed of filling those strong arms myself. And Quinn, with his rich voice and those black MacVie eyes, well he, too, set my heart to race. But 'tis Rory the lassies must watch out for — eyes like the summer sky. He's a good lad, but a rake to be sure. The one who amazed me the most was the youngest brother, Ian. What a sight he was. He stood nearly a head taller than Jack, taller even than Alec. His red hair blazed like fire, falling past his chest, too. His eyes were as blue as Rory's, and he was such a lamb, always asking if I needed help and telling me to sit and rest while he cleared the table after dinner. I've never met a sweeter lad. And I said as much to Jack, and do ye know what he told me?"

Captivated, Joanie shook her head in response, the bannocks completely forgotten.

"He said that Ian was the kindest of the lot, but that he became a beast when provoked. 'Tis the red hair, Jack said. To this day, I can't imagine Ian's countenance any other way than gentle, but I reckon given his height and the breadth of his shoulders, he would be a chilling sight if provoked."

"I assume ye're talking about Ian."

Joanie whirled around and looked at Alec who she had not heard enter. "Is it true?" she asked.

"Indeed, it is," Alec said. He came to her side and started to help her put the bannock in the basket. "But he never loses his temper for selfish reasons. 'Tis always in defense of injustice. He is a champion to anyone he deems is in need."

"What about your sister, Rose?" Joanie asked.

A shadow crossed Alec's features as a sad smile curved his lips. "Rose is the real MacVie in charge. She's strong and kind, always quick to laugh."

"What is it?" Joanie asked, placing her hand on his arm. "There is something you're not saying."

"'Tis hard to speak of," Alec said.

Helena cleared her throat, coming to stand next to them. "I'll do it so ye don't have to, Alec." Then she turned her gentle eyes on Joanie. "Rose's husband and three daughters were killed during the massacre."

Joanie's hand flew to her mouth.

Helena's arm came around her shoulders. "I ken, sweetling. Graver circumstances are hard to imagine, but Rose pushes on and so shall we." She waved her spoon at the table. "Shall we eat?"

Joanie's stomach growled.

Alec pulled her close, then turned to Helena. "I believe ye have yer answer."

They sat together at the table, passing food and sharing stories and concerns. All the while, Joanie sat quietly but listened with her whole heart. Alec asked Hamish about the farm. They spoke of the approaching springtime and preparing for the plant. Helena regaled them with a tale of how their goats had made their way into a neighboring croft and ate half the owners' straw mattress."

"I told ol' Betty that now she didn't have to suffer through Finnean's cold feet in the night," Helena said, throwing her head back with laughter.

Joanie loved every word, every burst of laughter, every warm glance. She loved the smell of hot pottage, the sweet, honeyed mead, and the coziness of the blazing hearth. With a full and grateful heart, she returned Helena's hug and Hamish's warm smile.

"Did ye enjoy supper?" Alec asked after their hosts had retired to their bed.

She smiled. "You know I did."

"I ken, but I just wanted to hear of yer pleasure from yer own lips."

Joanie cupped his cheek. "I loved it," she said and pressed a soft kiss to his lips.

"Me as well," he said, pulling her close. He stroked a finger down her cheek. "Although I'm lamenting our lack of privacy," he whispered.

She swallowed the laughter that bubbled up her throat. Then together, they shooed the goats away, rolled out a pallet, and laid down. Alec held her while the rain battered the rooftop and thunder cracked. Lightning flashed through the shuttered windows.

Joanie sighed and closed her eyes, feeling perfectly content, and she thought how wonderful it was to be indoors, secure within the arms of the man she loved, on such a terrible night. Her eyes flew open, and she realized the truth of her thoughts. She loved Alec. She loved him with every breath in her body, with her entire being. She could not imagine a life without him at her side. Yes, she wholeheartedly loved Alec MacVie.

"I love ye too," he whispered in her ear, pulling her close.

Tears filled her eyes. She turned into him, wrapping her arms around his neck. Surrounded by love and warmth, she fell into a deep, dreamless sleep.

Chapter Twenty Four

After they bid farewell to Hamish and Helena, Alec set their mare on course along a swiftly moving river.

Alec stroked Rosie's neck. "She's tired of all this walking and needs a good rest."

Joanie stiffened in her seat. "We're going to town then?"

"Aye, it cannot be avoided, but Dunshire is a quiet hamlet."

Joanie stretched her neck from side to side, like she had seen him do from time to time and straightened in her seat. "Then we go to town," she said resolutely.

The river wound through glades of wood and cut across open fields, swelling over boulders in a crescendo of white, then tumbling down into a crystal loch, which marked the beginning of Dunshire. From the high ground, Joanie scanned the numerous cottages, huts, and market stalls in the distance.

"Are ye ready?" he asked.

Joanie nodded absently as she gazed upon the large church that dominated the small hamlet. "What church is that?" she asked, hand to forehead to shield her eyes from the sun.

"'Tis no simple church. 'Tis Glenrose Abbey."

The sun shone high overhead as they descended the hill.

"Look," Joanie said, laughing while she pointed to a band of young girls running after a flock of wild ducks. They likely had just touched down to greet the approaching spring. The girls were no older than six or seven. They raced after each other, laughing with arms stretched out to the sunshine. Joy, freedom, and love radiated from their smiles, from their tangled hair, and stained tunics. They were a part of the world as much as the trees and the rocks, and they knew it.

Joanie cupped her hand over her lips, a surge of tears surprising her as she watched the girls disappear down the hill and into Dunshire. She drew a shaky breath and turned her face to the sun, savoring its powerful kiss on her cheeks. Straining her head back, the heat caressed her neck. She took a deep breath and smiled through the tears that continued to wet her cheeks. The promise of spring was in the air. Little green shoots peeked through the lusterless bracken, roots searching for their fruit and flower, aching to break free from the cold earth that had held them captive for so long.

She sat even straighter then and untied her cloak, letting it puddle around her waist. She reached up and took the pins from her hair, releasing it, and letting it tumble down her back, the same as the little girls, wild and free. Warm currents of air lifted her hair, and she tossed her head back and raised her arms, straining to reach the sky, the sun, the white clouds, the birds. In that moment of extravagance, she knew with her whole heart that she, too, was part of the world, that she had as much right to be there as anyone else. She was the same as the birds above and as the flowers that would soon rise again from their snowy grave — and so would she.

Suddenly, the horse came to a halt. "Go," Alec urged. "Do what it is in yer heart."

Her feet hit the ground before she had any time to think, and she ran, arms outstretched. She raced the rest of the way down the hill, the wind whipping through her unbound hair, and when she reached the bottom, she spun around and around, her arms stretching to the sky. She felt like she could fly, like she could do anything. She stopped breathless and stared up at a single bird circling overhead. It was so small and yet it could float like an angel in the heavens. She thought of all the times she had bent, yielding to another's will. How many people had looked at her like she was nothing, like she was worthless? They had beaten her, hurt her... She fisted her hands and put her head back and raged — a roar from the very depths of her soul, expelling the fear they had planted within her. No longer would she carry the yoke of another's disdain. Her life would no longer be a desperate struggle for survival. Her life mattered.

"Never again," she said, vowing to herself.

"Ye're amazing," Alec said behind her. And in that moment, she believed him.

"I'm done being afraid."

He swung down from the horse and knelt in front of her. Pulling her close, he pressed the side of his face against her chest. Then he looked up. "You will never have the need," he vowed.

She lowered her head and cupped his cheeks. "I feel like I am seeing the world for the first time, and it is you who has opened my eyes." She pressed her hand to her chest. "I give you my heart."

His hands came under her arms, and he stood, sweeping her high in the air above his head. His black eyes shone and a smile so wide it made her heart ache stretched across his beautiful face. Then he slowly lowered his arms until she was pressed against him, her toes grazing the earth. "Marry me," he said. "Be my wife."

Her heart pounded in her chest, "Yes," she cried out, throwing her head back.

Alec kissed her neck and held her in his arms and let her tears and laughter wash over him, cleansing him from the inside out. For so long, he had lived a half-life — head down and unfeeling, afraid of what he might see or hear if he looked ahead. The world around him came into focus with her at his side. The strength of her heart shielded his own, even from his own powers.

"I love ye, Joanie, so fiercely, so completely."

She reached high and cupped his cheeks, pulling his lips down to meet hers. Boldly, she kissed him with a hunger that fed his starved soul. He groaned when her tongue slowly traced his bottom lip and her hands splayed wide on his chest.

"I want to see you," she said breathlessly. "I have longed for you."

Her words scorched him, setting his whole being on fire. He swept his arm beneath her legs and carried her back toward a thick patch of wood, his lips never leaving hers.

She groaned in protest when her feet touched the brittle earth, and his lips tore from hers. He swept his cloak from his shoulders, laying it on ground. Even though he no longer touched her, currents of heat pulsed from his body, filling her, caressing her, feeding the ache that burned within her. A breath later, his hands grabbed her waist, crushing her against his. His lips seized hers, forceful and strong. She moaned as his tongue stoked hers, the heat within her building. She fumbled with the buckle hanging low on his hips, wishing to touch his skin. He unclasped his belt and yanked his tunic over his head. Her hands stretched wide against his smooth, snowy white skin. He burned like fire, the heat coursing through her fingers, stroking her feverishly from the inside out. Desire drove her impatient fingers to push his low-slung hose even lower. Lean, defined muscles shifted beneath her fingertips as he grabbed her close and stole her breath with his kiss.

The very taste of her consumed him, he could not satiate his desire to kiss and lick and suckle every inch of her beautiful body fast enough. He whisked her tunic over her head. Her shift followed just as quickly. His eyes drank in the sight of her small, pert breasts, her narrow waist and the gentle flare of her hips. He stroked his hand down her side, following the curve of her shape. His caress continued to her back. Then he cupped her soft round buttocks and thrust her against him. The sound of her fiery moan drove him wild with hunger. She surrounded him, her own pleasure filling him as he felt what she felt. Her body, her touch, her smell, her taste. She brought him to the very brink of control, provoking the feral animal within his soul. He needed their bodies to be one.

Her whole body burned, the ache building, throbbing, climbing. She wove her fingers through his long, black hair as she kissed him with total abandon, her tongue tasting, stroking, teasing. Her nails tore at his skin as her desperation grew. He dropped to his knees, his mouth consuming her, first her taut nipples, then searing a path down her stomach. He pulled her down onto his warm cloak and spread her thighs wide. Cold air shocked and teased her sensitive flesh, but then his breath found the very heat of her. She cried out, arching her back as his tongue stroked her, circling her sensitive nub, before plunging inside her. Heat surged through her, fierce, possessive, undulating, endless. She cried out again as pleasure and painful yearning melded into hot, torturous need. Her body demanded fulfillment.

His body, his heart, the hard length of him throbbed for her. His soul burned. The taste of her honeyed warmth intoxicated his senses, blurring his mind and heart until he did not exist — only hunger, only desire remained. He stretched his body over hers, groaning when her legs surrounded his waist, and he eased slowly inside her slick, tight warmth. Her innocence shattered around him. She cried out, her nails tearing his back. He felt her pain. He hovered over her, shaking, waiting for her relief, and when it came, he slowly thrust deeper. Her desire flamed, licking his own, stroking the fire burning inside him. He felt her need. He felt her pleasure, heightening his own pleasure until he thought he would burst from the power pulsing from her body into his. He thrust deeper, harder. Her moans and pleas echoed like thunder in his mind. And then her body seized. Her heart quaked. She shuddered as wave after wave of pleasure rocked her body, igniting his own desperate need. They clung to each other. Together, their bodies and souls quaked and shattered into oblivious euphoria.

Branches tangled overhead. She stared at the maze of limbs, her body and mind drained of everything but hazy pleasure. They laid together, their own limbs as entwined as the trees above long after they had caught their breath and quieted their racing hearts. It was not until Alec felt a chill enter Joanie's body that he reached for her tunic and helped her dress.

They walked the rest of the way to the village, hand in hand. When they stepped among the cottages, the din of activity reaching them, Alec kissed her slowly, passionately before he started to pull her a little behind him.

"No," she said gently. She saw the world in his eyes when he looked at her. She saw his love and her greatness — all visible deep inside his knowing black eyes.

"After you," he said with a smile.

Back straight, shoulders back, she walked out in front of him and took his hand, leading him through the streets without a trace of fear in her heart.

Chapter Twenty Five

The small hamlet of Dunshire had but one stable with only half a dozen horses, none of which matched Rosie in terms of strength or health. Still, Alec considered each beast and chose a black stallion who, although past his prime, he felt had plenty of heart left.

After making the stable master very happy over the trade, Alec brought the horse to the smithy to be reshod, leaving Joanie to wander the small market. At first, he wanted to deny her the independence, to keep her protected and safe at his side. But he also knew that her own safety and wellbeing relied first on her believing in herself.

After visiting the market himself, he caught up with her sometime later. He found her sitting on the far side of the village green, nibbling a small meat pie and staring up at the abbey, situated on higher ground beyond the outskirts of the village proper.

"Would ye like to go inside?" he asked as he walked up to her.

She nodded brightly. "I've never been inside an abbey."

He held out his hand to her, and together they walked the stone inlaid path up to the tall, arched doors of Glenrose, which led into the chapel. The air was cold and thick with incense. Stained-glass windows composed of somber faces, which contrasted with radiant innumerable colors, lined one side. Rays of sunlight reached through the glass, casting beams of colors across the floor. Joanie slowly walked through the shafts of light, smiling as the colors danced across her tunic.

Alec fell back and watched her, intoxicated by the sight of her pleasure. Then he stiffened, feeling someone approach. Turning, he looked expectantly at the door near the Sacristy. A moment later, a tall, slim priest entered. His youthful face was open and kind, and his shorn red hair glinted with different colors as he walked along the wall with the stained-glass windows.

"Greetings, my children," he said, dipping his head to both Alec and Joanie. "The next Mass is not for another hour."

Alec immediately let his guard down. He softened his eyes and posturing. The clergy, whose lives truly were devoted to God, had always put him at ease. From the start, Alec and Abbot Matthew's relationship had been effortless. The abbot's emotions seldom ran wild, and he never tried to understand Alec. He was with Alec as he was with everyone — mindful, heartfelt, and without judgment. The priest standing in front of him bore his rank with the same ease and looked at them without judgment or expectation. Alec dipped his head in return. "We did not come for Mass." Then he smiled at Joanie. "We have something else in mind."

Joanie raised a quizzical brow at him. He smiled and cupped her cheek. Looking into her eyes, he said to the priest. "We would like to be married."

The priest cleared his throat. "This is rather unconventional. What of her father? Have ye his permission?"

Alec turned then. "Our parents are dead. There is no one's permission to seek."

The priest's eyes shifted from Alec to Joanie. Smiling, he said, "I am Father Giles."

"My name is Alec MacVie. It is a pleasure to meet ye. I am a special friend to the Abbot of Haddington Abbey."

A flicker of recognition lit Father Giles's eyes, and Alec felt a sudden rush of warmth within the priest and knew he was aware of the cause.

Joanie stepped forward then. "I am Joanie Picard," she said confidently.

A warm smile spread across Father Giles's face. "Blessings, Joanie." Then he posed a question to them both. "Why do ye seek to marry?"

"She saved my life," Alec said simply.

Joanie slid her hand in his. "And he saved mine."

Father Giles smiled. "I have never known earthly love, but from my observations when two people truly fall in love, it is always because they are saving each other from the world. We all need saving in this life and the next. I found my salvation within these walls, and now ye find yers in each other's arms."

Then he swept his arm toward the front of the chapel. "Let us go to the altar."

"Wait," Alec said to Joanie, and from within his satchel he produced a long, gauzy veil and a crown of wildflowers, which he had just bought at the market.

"So beautiful," Joanie gasped.

Alec smiled as he swept the veil over her long black waves and fitted the crown on her head. He cupped her face. "Indeed, ye are."

Walking arm and arm, they joined Father Giles in front of the altar.

"We stand before ye, Lord, to unite these two hearts and in doing so, make them one, one love to last all eternity."

The priest's words filled Joanie's ears like the sweet refrain of a song, timeless and truthful. Currents of warmth flowed from Alec, filling her soul to the brim with unconditional love and acceptance. They spoke their vows to each other, quietly and clearly. And when Father Giles declared them husband and wife, Joanie threw her arms around Alec's neck just as he lifted her feet off the ground and sealed the promise of their vows with a kiss.

With his arm around her waist, they walked back through the chapel, multi-colored lights from the stained-glass windows dancing across her lovely face. Then a feeling struck Alec, and his eyes were pulled toward a door.

"Where does that lead?"

"'Tis the dormitory for our lay brothers," Father Giles replied.

Leaving Joanie, Alec crossed the room, not waiting for permission from the priest to proceed. His hand touched the latch on the door. Suddenly, a vision of English knights riding toward the abbey flashed in his mind's eyes. White tunics covered their armor, bearing the blood red cross of the Templar brotherhood. Pushing the door wide, he stormed down the hallway passing doorways on the left. He opened several, each a sparsely furnished cell. He opened another door, again taking in the thin pallet on the floor and the small rough-hewn table with a single stool. Every room was the same. He moved down to the next door and clasped the latch and was struck by sudden fear, raw and urgent, but it was not his fear.

He swung the door wide and stood in awe at what he saw. The room matched the others, a simple pallet, table, and stool. But upon the smooth stone wall, stretching from floor to ceiling, was a painting, breathtaking in its vibrancy, of an angel in flowing blue robes with eyes that burned like fire, and in his hand, he gripped a long, slim, golden trumpet. Radiating from his flaxen head were streaks of light that caressed myriad stars and clouds in a heavenly sky.

He heard Joanie gasp as she entered. Tearing his eyes away from the angel's face, he reached for her, pulling her close. His heart still pounding under the weight of need burning his soul straight from the angel's fiery gaze.

Father Giles entered the small cell. "I see ye've found Brother Ambrose's room."

"Where is he?" Alec asked, not bothering to conceal the urgency in his voice. "I must speak with him."

A sad look crossed the priest's features. "If only I knew. He is one of seven of our brothers who disappeared several years ago now."

Again, the flash of approaching soldiers came unbidden to his mind, only this time with blades drawn. "Did he perish when the abbey was attacked?"

"The abbey has fallen victim to English raids in recent years, but that is not how we lost Brother Ambrose. He and the others may very well be alive for all we know. One night, they retired to their rooms, and in the morning, they were gone."

"There is something ye're not telling me."

Father Giles simply nodded. "There is a mystery surrounding Brother Ambrose, but I can assure ye 'tis not known to me. I took over the priestly duties in the chapel just two years ago.

My predecessor only bade me keep the room empty and never to alter the painting."

"Who is he?" Joanie asked, coming forward and gently running her fingers over the angel's bright blue robes.

"We believe he is Saint Gabriel."

Joanie whirled around, her eyes darting between Alec and the priest. "Saint Gabriel? I've heard of that?"

Father Giles chuckled. "Of course ye have, my child. He was the angel who visited the Blessed Virgin to tell her of the coming of our Savior, Jesus."

"No," Joanie said. "What I meant to say is that St. Gabriel is the name of the village in Scotland from which my grandmother hailed."

Alec could not believe it. "But that is only a few days ride from here. Why did ye not say so before?"

A grave expression shaped her face. "My grandmother is dead. There is no reason for me to go there."

Alec cupped her cheek. "But Joanie, don't ye ken ye could have other family there?"

Joanie gave pause. "My grandmother never spoke of family. I only know of St. Gabriel because of a song she taught me. It was a mournful song about angels crying."

The priest spoke up then. "St. Gabriel was once remade in grief. More than forty years ago, it was called Dàn Run, but tragically, a horrific scourge moved through the town, a mysterious malady that took most of the village's children up to heaven. As I was told, one of the craftsmen in the village, who had lost all five of his children, carved an effigy of Saint Gabriel, which he positioned at the gate to the graveyard. Just as Saint Gabriel had told Mary of the coming of the baby Jesus, he prayed Gabriel would tell God of the coming of their children. From that day on, the village of Dàn Run became known as Saint Gabriel."

"Thank you, Father Giles," Alec said abruptly, clasping Joanie's hand and hastening from the room.

"Go in peace," the priest called out behind them.

"What is it?" Joanie asked as she studied Alec's hard, deter-mined profile.

"I do not know," he said. Stopping, he withdrew the shard from around his neck. "But feel this."

Joanie's eyes widened in surprise as she wrapped her fingers around the stone. It was warmer than she'd ever felt it. "What does it mean?" she gasped.

He shook his head. "I do not know, but we are going to Saint Gabriel."

Chapter Twenty Six

"Will you tell me again about the Harborage?" Joanie asked as she followed on foot behind Alec through the dark woods.

"'Tis a safe place for Scotland's rebels, like Mary's inn in London, but the Harborage is an Eden with a clear pool within a wide-open glade, surrounded by tall dense trees. And built within several of those trees are beds high off the ground."

Alec led the way through tall Scots pines, their path ever twisting and turning.

"Are you certain you know where we are going?"

He glanced back at her, his full lips pursed together slightly and raised his brow.

"Oh," she said, smiling. Following behind, she admired her husband's broad shoulders and confident bearing.

He stopped and closed his eyes. "We are nearly there, but we are not alone."

"What do you mean? Who else could be out here?"

"Other agents, of course."

Thick pines gave way to slender birch trees. She listened to the song of a bubbling stream while she picked her way behind Alec. They followed the briskly flowing waters into a wide glade. Her eyes were first pulled toward a pool on the far side where a large man floated peacefully on the surface. Then her eyes darted to where another man lay, resting beneath a tree. Then she spotted one more building a fire.

"Do you know these men?" she whispered. Then she sucked in a sharp breath as the man in the pool suddenly stood. He wore naught but his hose. Water sluiced down his massive chest. His honey-colored hair clung to his shoulders. And he smiled when he saw them.

"By all the Saints, is that ye, Alec?" the man exclaimed.

All the men turned to look at them. A flash of surprise shaped their features before they stood and started to approach.

Joanie kept her eyes trained nervously on the largest man, nearly naked, dripping wet, and bearing down on them. He narrowed his eyes on Alec. Joanie glanced up and saw Alec, looking the man hard in the eye, the corners of his lips upturned.

"Grab yer blades, lads. He may look like Alec, but I believe 'tis a smile he's wearing."

One of the men scrambled for his sword, and the large man threw his head back laughing. "'Twas a jest, Paul." And then he was upon them, larger than life. A smile spread across his face, lighting up his blue eyes. He didn't say another word, but tentatively offered Alec his hand.

Alec accepted. "How are ye, Ramsay?"

Ramsay's eyes widened, then he threw back his head and whooped to the sky. Wrapping his big arms around Alec, pinning his arms to his sides, he squeezed him in a hard embrace. When he set Alec back down again, another man came forward. He had wavy blond hair, which reached his shoulders and green eyes. He, too, looked at Alec in disbelief and offered his hand, which Alec squeezed.

"Hello, David," Alec said.

David smiled but did not return Alec's greeting. Instead, he turned to Ramsay and asked, "Do ye think this is the work of the devil?"

Ramsay slowly shook his head, setting his gaze on Joanie. "Nay, 'tis an angel who brought Alec back to life." He bowed low, then smiled at her. "I believe 'tis safe to assume 'tis ye who has managed to put a smile on Alec's face."

Joanie blushed and pressed closer to Alec. He smiled down at her, then looked back to the men. "Joanie, this is Ramsay. He is a blacksmith and runs the Iron Shoe Tavern, a secret meeting room in his cellar that's just for agents, equipped with the finest ale ye'll ever taste. And this is David, a good agent and a good friend. Lads, meet my wife, Joanie." He turned back to her and said softly, "Joanie MacVie."

She smiled, hearing her new name for the first time.

"Wife?" Ramsay exclaimed. "When did this happen?"

Alec smiled. "A few hours ago."

Ramsay gave Alec a good-natured slap on the back. "Did ye hear that, lads. They've just been wed. We must celebrate." But then Ramsay looked down at his own bare chest, and he winked at Joanie. "First, I'll make myself decent."

Joanie watched Ramsay retreat across the glade. She could not believe how large he was. He was as tall as Alec, but much brawnier with his blacksmith's arms.

"Congratulations," David said with a bow.

Then another young man named Paul with chestnut brown hair and youthful eyes came forward, and smiling warmly, he bent and kissed her cheek. She blushed and turned away. By doing so, she noticed another man for the first time standing alone on the other side of the pool. He was handsome with dark hair and eyes, but he looked as hard and unpleasant as Randolph Tweed. Where once she might have shrunk behind Alec, she met his stony glare without flinching.

Alec dipped his head to the man in greeting before he walked Joanie over to where a large fire crackled and sputtered. "That is Nick," Alec whispered in her ear. "Forgive his coldness. He isn't a bad man. He lost his family during the same attack that claimed the lives of my own parents and sister. He grieves with a heart so full of hate that there is room for little else."

Four log benches surrounded the fire. Alec and Joanie sat down opposite David and Paul.

"Welcome to the harborage," Ramsay said, joining them clad in a black tunic. He handed out mugs of ale before he took his seat on the other side of Joanie. He looked over her head at Alec. "Since ye brought her here, can I assume she knows who we are."

"*Alba gu bràth*," Joanie burst out, speaking for the first time.

Ramsay threw his head back with laughter, and Paul raised his cup in the air, "*Alba gu bràth*." But an angry growl cut through the gaiety as Nick stormed toward them, drawing his sword.

"Ye brought an English woman to the Harborage," he hissed.

Alec and the others shot to their feet, shielding Joanie from Nick's wrath.

Joanie's heart pounded as she glanced up at Alec's hard eyes and stony face.

"I have brought my wife to the harborage," he said simply, his voice steady. He held Nick's gaze, locked in battle, then his eyes softened. "Yer shame hurts ye far more than yer grief."

Joanie flinched as Nick bared his teeth at Alec. "Ye're the one who should feel ashamed, bringing the enemy to this sacred place."

Alec continued, speaking quietly and clearly. "Ye're not to blame for yer family's death."

Nick growled and lunged at Alec but was stopped by Ramsay's mighty arm. "Do not speak to me of my family," he shouted.

"Ye're not to blame for yer family's death," Alec said in the same calm tone.

"I ken I'm not to blame," Nick snarled. "English soldiers burned my wife and my three children alive in the very home I made for them."

"Aye," Alec said, his voice still low, "but ye blame yerself for being alive when they are not. Ye blame yerself for not protecting them, even though there was no way ye could have."

Nick's nostrils flared. "I could have been home," he shouted, his voice cracking at the end. He dropped his arms to his sides, his sword slipping from his limp fingers. Tears flooded his eyes. "I could've refused the commission on that ship."

"Then how would ye have fed them?" Alec continued softly. "A man must labor to feed his family. Ye did nothing wrong, Nick. Ye were a good husband, a good father, and a good provider." He stepped forward, still holding Nick's gaze. "Justice and vengeance are not the same. We seek justice with our cause, for yer family, for all Scotland's families, but ye surrender yer soul to them with yer hate."

Nick's face twisted with rage as he glared at Alec. "Do not cast yer demon-seeing eyes on me." His fists clenched. Joanie thought he might burst from everything building and brewing within him. He turned away from Alec's compassion and raised his fists to the heavens where his wife and young children awaited him. A bellow, raw and vulnerable, tore from his lips in a fury to reach them. Then he dropped to his knees, a sob wracking his shoulders.

Joanie understood pain. His cry cut straight through her heart. She knelt beside him and wrapped her arms around him. He turned his face into her neck and wept.

Alec's chest flooded with warmth at the sight of his fearless and compassionate wife, comforting a man who only moments before had threatened her life. He watched as she stroked Nick's back. He could feel Joanie's healing touch at work calming Nick's weary and heartbroken soul. Only she could bring him peace with naught but her soothing, powerful hand and wounded, knowing heart.

After a while, Nick sat back and wiped a hand across his eyes. "I've been a fool," he muttered.

Joanie cupped his cheek with her hand. "No one should have to suffer the way you have."

Alec reached down and offered Nick his hand. "Remember the abbot's teaching: darkness can never extinguish the light. Yer family is always with ye."

"Forgive me," Nick said.

Alec shook his head. "There is naught to forgive."

Alec held Joanie's hand and led her back to the log. When Nick took a seat next to Paul, Paul made the sign of the cross, and David blew out a long, slow breath, and said, "Jesus, Alec, in all the years that we've stayed here and ye kept to yerself, I've often wondered what it would be like to have ye join us around the fire. Dispelling demons is not what I imagined."

Alec turned and looked at David. "Do ye want to be next?"

"Have at me." David said.

"The lass who works at the tavern in Dunshire is not going to wait for ye forever."

David's eyes widened in surprise. Then he raised his cup to Alec. "I ken."

"Me next," Paul said, smiling.

"Ye're a pup. Yer heart has never been broken. It will not always be so. Enjoy yer pleasant dreams while ye may."

"What about me?" Ramsay said, crossing his thick blacksmith's arms over his chest.

Alec smiled slightly and shook his head. "I wouldn't dare."

"Good man," Ramsay said. He took a long draught of ale before he asked. "So how did ye two meet?"

Alec felt Joanie stiffen at his side. Ramsay's questions stirred a place of deep sadness within her, sadness for her own trials but mostly, her grief for Diana. He wrapped his arm around her waist, pulling her close. "I heard her sing and knew hers was the only song I ever wanted to hear again."

"I would love to hear ye," Nick said quietly.

Ramsay raised his cup. "The harborage has never been graced with music."

"This is supposed to be a celebration," Paul said, smiling at Joanie.

Alec looked down at Joanie whose cheeks were tinted a lovely pink. "We are in the Highlands," he said softly. "'Tis time to bring yer music home." He felt her elation growing inside of her.

Joanie looked straight ahead and closed her eyes. "This song was taught to me by my grandmother. May God rest her soul."

When the first note left her lips, it unleashed a flood of emotions. Today, she had felt the kiss of the sun and Alec's warm hands on her naked body. She had married him, sharing sacred vows before an altar, wearing a crown of wildflowers. She had comforted the broken heart of a Scottish rebel, and she had longed for her own beloved Diana. And all these moments—some glorious, others sad but all achingly beautiful — she surrendered to her song. The notes welled from her heart and crooned off her tongue, coiling around the men, then up through the trees. She imagined her voice being carried on the Highland wind, welcomed by the trees, the stars above, the earth beneath her feet like an old friend. The story she told was of that land, a story of a young Scottish lass who loved a sailor and awaited his return for seven long years, fearing he was lost forever.

Joanie poured her own heartache into the lass's longing. And when the lass spied his ship on the horizon, Joanie imbued the words with her own joy and wonderment in finding Alec. The final note grazed the treetops, high and soft as a caress, then faded to breath.

She opened her eyes. Nick, Ramsay, David, and Paul stared at her with unmistakable looks of wonder and admiration. Blushing, she turned into Alec and hid her face for a moment before she smiled.

Ramsay raked his hand through his long blond hair. "Wow."

David blew out a long breath, then pressed his hands on his knees and stood. "All right, then. I'll be back before dawn," he said and grabbed his satchel and sword and disappeared into the woods.

"Where is he going?" Paul asked.

"To the tavern in Dunshire," Alec said, one side of his lips lifting in a sideways grin. "There's a lass he needs to see."

"Are ye going to tell us what the two of ye are doing here on yer wedding night?" Ramsay asked before taking a bite of dried meat.

Nick nodded. "Why are ye not still at the palace?"

"Edward's men arrived," Alec said.

The sip of ale Paul had just taken sprayed from his lips. "Do ye think he knows about the stolen treasure?"

Alec nodded. "When the keeper discovered what happened, he sent word of the robbery."

Ramsay shrugged. "Calm yerself, Paul. No one could suspect it was us."

"We do not exist, remember?" Alec said to Paul. "Anyway, I was planning on leaving London," he said, putting his hand on Joanie's knee.

Ramsay smiled knowingly. "If ye wait to steal a prize like Joanie, ye may wind up empty handed."

"Oh, he didn't steal me," Joanie said, trying to keep from smiling. "He bought me for one-hundred silver marks."

Once more, ale sprayed from Paul's lips.

Nick leaned forward. "All right, from the beginning then, Alec."

Alec smiled and wrapped his arm protectively around Joanie. He certainly had no intention of imparting Joanie's personal struggles to his friends. "Do not think that just because I'm sitting with ye around a fire that I'm going to tell ye all my secrets."

Paul laughed. "It seems only fair, since ye know all of ours."

"Nay, yer story is yer own," Ramsay said. "But I am interested to know where ye're heading now?"

"Joanie's grandmother hailed from St. Gabriel. We are going to see if she has any family left there." Alec stood then and offered his hand to Joanie. "If ye'll excuse us now, we plan to set out early in the morning."

"Not to mention it is yer wedding night," Ramsay said.

Alec wrapped his arm around Joanie's waist and led her from the fire.

"*Alba gu bràth*," Ramsay called after them.

The other men responded in unison. "*Alba gu bràth*," before draining their cups.

Joanie followed Alec through the thick trees and gasped with delight when he pointed to their bed for the night. A wooden platform stuck out halfway up the tree. She climbed a rope ladder with Alec just behind her. And when they reached the top, he pulled the ladder up into a neat pile. Surrounding the platform was a protective railing. Joanie gazed out from their perch, delighted by the view.

"This is magnificent," she said.

He smiled and nodded. "It was my favorite place in the world."

She looked at him curiously. "Where is your favorite place now?"

He pulled her close, bringing his lips a breath away from hers. "Wherever ye are," he whispered. Then his lips claimed hers. Her arms flew around his neck. She returned his kiss with a demand all her own, a hunger gripping her body, a hunger that could never be sated even if they lived a century in each other's arms.

"I need you now," she gasped. "I need you always."

Alec eased her tunic and shift over her head and hungrily pulled first one rosy nipple into his mouth, then the other. Her hands coursed over his body, searching, wanting. Then he felt her fingers pulling on his hose. He deepened his kiss as he freed himself. She stared up at him, her limpid eyes half closed with desire that surged from her body into his. Parting her legs, her arms reached for him. He stretched over her, his hand cupped her breast, his thumb gently teasing her hard peak, eliciting soft moans from her wet, parted lips. Then his hand caressed down her sleek torso, then lower still. Unable to resist her heat, his fingers gently grazed her soft folds. She writhed beneath him, arching her back, thrusting her hips. He deepened his touch, stroking her, feeling her hunger, her need, her body telling him exactly what it wanted. The instant before her mounting pleasure erupted, he shifted over her and thrust into her, deep and hard. She shattered around him, coaxing his own pleasure to crest and soar. He thrust into her harder and deeper until he seized for a moment, a breath. Then wave after wave of pleasure rocked through him into her.

Chapter Twenty Seven

Alec opened his eyes and reached for the sword above his head. He sat up the instant before he heard someone shout his name.

Joanie jolted awake. "What's going on?"

"'Tis David," Alec said, pushing aside the blankets. "Come," he said as he started down the ladder. He helped Joanie to the ground, then they hurried through the trees and into the clearing. Scowling, David stood in the middle of the glade, his feet planted wide, and in his fist, he gripped a large piece of rolled up parchment.

Alec narrowed his eyes on the parchment and let go of Joanie's hand as he stormed across the clearing and took the scroll from David's outstretched hand. Unraveling it, he scanned the page and found his own eyes staring back at him. A moment later, Ramsay, Nick, and Paul appeared at his side. He gave Ramsay the scroll.

"What is it?" Joanie asked, arriving breathless at his side.

He erected his walls to shield her from his anger before he turned and showed her the image. "It is a likeness of me."

She gasped and grabbed the parchment from Ramsay's hand, her eyes scouring the page, apprehension and confusion pouring off her in pulsing waves.

She looked up at him, her face stricken. "I cannot read."

He didn't want her to know.

"What does it say?" she snapped.

There had to be a way to spare her.

"Someone tell me," she cried, her eyes darted from face to face. He could feel the panic building within her.

"I am wanted for the robbery of the King's Chapter House, or at least Randolph Tweed is."

The parchment dropped from her fingertips as shock set in. "Joanie, breathe," he said firmly as he pulled her into his arms.

"I don't understand," David said. "How could ye be accused? No one could possibly suspect any of us."

"That's just it," Alec began, "no one does suspect me. 'Tis Randolph Tweed who stands accused."

Joanie looked up at him, her brows drawn. "But the keeper favors you. I ... I was standing right there when he said so."

"He did," Alec said softly. "But the keeper's palace, the palace ye knew, disappeared the moment Edward's soldiers returned. John's life is forfeit. The missing treasure is only one of several charges he will no doubt face, although the Chapter House robbery will certainly be the gravest charge. Edward's man would have demanded answers. He would have wanted names."

"But why would John accuse you?" Joanie asked.

"I doubt he did, but if someone else accused me, I do not believe John would have championed me when his own neck was on the line."

"Geoffrey," she gasped.

Alec nodded.

"Who is Geoffrey?" Ramsay asked.

"My old master," Joanie muttered. "The one Alec paid one-hundred silver marks for my freedom."

"'Tis a small fortune ye paid this man. Why would he turn on ye?" Nick asked.

"Because the coin I paid him I later stole back." He turned to Joanie. "We must go."

"Alec, ye ken they are likely spreading these in every tavern, ale house, and village green in Scotland. And look at the price on yer head."

Joanie's eyes widened. "You didn't say there was a price on your head. What is the amount, Ramsay?"

"One-hundred silver marks, an amount I'm certain is no coincidence," Ramsay said, then turned to Alec. "I will need just a minute to gather my affects."

Alec shook his head. "Ye needn't come along. I ken ye're supposed to return to Haddington. Brother Matthew will want yer report."

"Brother Matthew will want us to stand with our brother."

"Ramsay's right," David said. "Ye're a wanted man now. If ye still insist on going to Saint Gabriel, we're coming with ye."

Chapter Twenty Eight

Alec scanned the wooden wall that enclosed the village of Saint Gabriel. The village gate was open. The sun rose behind the hill, painting the soft clouds a dusky rose. He passed through the gate and glanced back at Ramsay, who sat astride a large charger, his broad sword strapped to his back. David and Nick both rode spotted mares. Paul had ridden on alone to Haddington to provide the abbot with a report.

The morning sun chased the chill from the air. By the time they passed through the gate, the sky was bright, and it was clear that the first breath of Spring had come to Saint Gabriel. People milled about, content to feel the sunshine on their faces for a change. Wet, soft earth scented the air. Birdsong combined with the din of voices and laughter.

"I can't believe we are here," Joanie whispered.

He pressed her tighter to his chest. "Ye don't feel afraid," he observed.

"I'm not. I'm..." She expelled a breath. "I can hardly say how I feel."

He pulled her closer. "Now, ye will at least know where she grew up."

She turned and glanced up at him. "Is it still hot?" she whispered.

"Like fire," Alec answered, knowing she meant the shard of stone. He was growing increasing excited. He did not doubt that the stone had led him to Joanie, and Joanie to Saint

Gabriel. For good or for ill, the stone's secret, mayhap Scotland's secret, would soon be revealed.

Alec closed his eyes and allowed his heart to guide them. They wandered alongside several cottages and the blacksmith's forge. Then they came to the village green.

"Look," Joanie said, pointing. "It's Saint Gabriel, just as Father Giles described."

A wooden statue, intricately carved, stood guard in front of a fenced-in graveyard. A sudden wave of sadness surged through Alec.

"But then that means all those graves are..." Joanie faltered.

Alec knew what she did not want to say out loud. Children, once so beloved, lay beneath the small crosses that dotted the ground, too numerous to count.

He turned away from the heartbreaking sight, his eyes settling on a young woman with red hair twisted in a knot on her head, and a thick shawl about her shoulders. On her ample hip, she carried a basket of laundry. Suddenly compelled, he followed her.

"Where are we going?" he heard Ramsay ask, but Alec kept his silence, unable to tear his eyes away. He had this incredible feeling of familiarity and warmth. At the edge of the green, she turned down a road that led behind a cluster of clay and thatch huts. Nudging his horse into a trot, he sped up after her, the urgency to find her growing stronger with each passing second. He turned the corner. His heart started to pound when he stared down an empty path, but then he glimpsed just the end of her shawl lifting in the breeze like a finger beckoning him before disappearing around another corner.

"What is it Alec?" Joanie breathed.

He heard her words, but he couldn't speak. He could only ride. His heart raced. He rounded the corner. And then he saw her. The young woman stood at the very end of the road where it stopped abruptly in front of a small stone cottage. Her laundry basket still sat on her wide hip. Who was she? Why was he so drawn to her? Mayhap, she was a relation of Joanie's. He carried on forward, but at a slower place, not wishing to alarm her. He watched intently as she set the basket down and swept the shawl from her shoulders. She stepped to the side, revealing an older woman sitting in a rough-hewn chair, her face downcast.

His breath caught. "It can't be."

"What is it?" Joanie asked.

The young woman swept the shawl around the older woman's shoulder. Slowly, the old woman looked up and smiled.

It felt like thunder erupted in his chest the moment Joanie saw her.

Joanie grabbed his hands, her nails digging into him. Her body seized, and a word began to take form, originating soul-deep. It surged through her body, cutting a searing path of agony and hope up her throat and she screamed, "Grandmother."

The woman jerked around. Her faded blue eyes grew wide, then she clasped a hand to her mouth and fell back into the chair. The young woman reached out to steady her. Gnarled fingers, splayed wide, reached out. "Joanie!"

Joanie jumped from the horse, the face she knew so well a blur through her tears. "Grandmother!"

"Joanie!"

Sobbing, Joanie fell to her knees and seized her grandmother's hands. Her aged body trembled and shook as tears coursed down her creased cheeks. Then Joanie flung her arms wide and pulled her into a tremulous embrace. Her softness, her smell, her breath, her feel, everything about her filled Joanie until there was no room inside her to breathe, or for her heart to beat. Joanie sobbed and sobbed, thinking she would surely die if she were to awaken and it was all a dream.

"Are you real?" Joanie cried, pulling back to see her grandmother's face. Still, her grandmother cried. She could only nod, her lips pressed wide, and she held Joanie tight. Joanie knew in her heart, in her soul that she was real.

She was alive!

Joanie faltered and pulled away. Her stomach dropped, and her blood ran cold.

Her grandmother was alive, which meant...

She had never died.

Fury, unbidden and undeniable, shot through her. Her hands clenched into tight fists as the ugly truth boiled to the surface of her heart.

"But he said you were dead," she gritted, squeezing her fists tighter. Rage like nothing she had ever known coursed through her. She couldn't breathe.

"He told me you were dead," she cried again. "He ... he ... buried you, and he..." She pressed the heels of her hands into her eyes, unable to find a way out of her anger. Then, suddenly, Alec's arms came around her.

"Put it in me," he breathed in her ear. "Give all yer rage to me."

She clung to him, squeezing him, tension riddling her body as she fought to see beyond her hatred for a father who could tell his daughter such a vicious lie.

"I am here."

Her grandmother's words slowly soothed their way into her mind. "I am here, sweetling."

Alec's heat soothed a path to her heart. She felt her grandmother rest her hand on her back. Slowly, the fury softened. She released her grip on Alec's tunic. Her shoulders fell away from her ears, and she turned in Alec's arms and beheld her grandmother's beautiful blue eyes, which crinkled when a smile spread across her face.

Pressing her lips together to hold back a fresh wave of tears, Joanie left Alec's arms and entered her grandmother's embrace. "There, there, sweetling. I'm here now," she crooned, just as she had when Joanie was a little girl.

Joanie lifted her head and whispered, "Alec, this is my grandmother, Margaret."

Chapter Twenty Nine

"Are you expecting someone, Grandmother?"

Smiling, her grandmother nodded. "Aye, my wee lamb should be home soon. He is my great nephew." She smiled and squeezed Joanie's hand. "Yer cousin. His mother died birthing him." Margaret closed her eyes. "Mira was such a kind-hearted lass. God rest her soul." She took a deep breath and opened her eyes. "Mira's mother, my own Bradana, passed away just last spring, and so Matthew became mine. He's an uncanny lad. Ye'll see," she said with a wink. "Anyway, what were we discussing? This mind of mine wanders."

"You were telling me about when my father first came to Saint Gabriel."

"Aye, now I see why I tried to forget. If I could erase Drogo forever from my mind I would. I'll tell ye, Joanie, I knew from the very first moment I laid eyes on him that he had a dark soul. He was the youngest son of a knight. His brothers became soldiers for hire and were eventually knighted, or so yer father claimed. But he chose a less honorable path. What I'm about to tell ye, I gleaned over the years, listening to his drunken babble. Drogo refused his father's help gaining a commission, and so he was given a modest fortune from his father's earnings to make his own way. As ye can very well imagine, he drank his way through the money easily enough and started running with a band of outlaws, eventually fleeing England a wanted man, which is how he came to discover St. Gabriel."

"If he was so awful, how could my mother have agreed to marry him, an outlaw and a drunk?"

"My Gavenia was too young to mind his deeds over his words. Also, in his youth yer father was a handsome and charming man. When he came here, no one knew his past. With his pockets lined with stolen coin, he beguiled his way into the hearts of many here in the village. Before anyone knew it, he had cheated them all, and worst of all, he had convinced my Gavenia to run away with him. Trust me, Joanie, I tried to reason with yer mother, but she was already under the spell of his blue eyes and fine smile." Her grandmother shook her head sadly. "He came to her like Lucifer himself, beautiful to look at but wicked to his core."

"How did ye learn of their plan to run away?" Alec asked.

Tears stung Margaret's eyes. Her hand flew to her chest against the pain of remembering. "I overheard them," she said weakly. "Gavenia could not be swayed. Bradana was already married then and to a good man. And so, I left her and Saint Gabriel behind and followed them. I had known men like Drogo before. I knew the vile deeds he was capable of. I wanted to do everything in my power to save her." Her faded blue eyes, glistening with tears, locked with Joanie's. "But I couldn't. Nor could I save ye."

Joanie squeezed her grandmother's hand. "What happened to you? What did he do to you?"

Margaret swiped at her tears. "Well, as ye know, I was ill. While ye were working at the tavern, he stuck me in the back of a wagon and drove north for several hours. Then he dumped me on the side of the road."

Joanie gasped, her hand to her heart.

"By the time I made it back to ye, ye were gone. He had sold ye." Margaret grabbed both of Joanie's hands. "I searched for ye for years. I lived off the charity of convents and searched every village I passed through. I..."

Joanie pulled her grandmother close. She stroked her curved back and whispered soothing words. "None of that matters anymore. It can't. He will win in the end if we don't let the past go."

Her grandmother pulled away and smiled up at her. "I never dreamed I would see ye again. And it does my heart good to see ye so well and happy," she said, turning to pat Alec's hand.

Alec smiled. "All is just as it should be," he said, and then he straightened in his seat. He had sensed the lad's presence the instant before the cottage door cracked open.

Margaret smiled and clasped her hands together. "Here's my wee lamb now."

A small boy of seven or eight years silently stepped into the cottage and shut the door behind him, then darted to Margaret's side, burying his face in her neck. "His name is Matthew."

"Good morrow," Joanie said.

Margaret stroked his sandy hair. "He doesn't speak. At least not yet. I think he can. I just don't think he has ever found something he thought truly worthy of saying."

Alec felt an immediate kinship with the lad. He stood and circled around the old woman and squatted down in front of Matthew.

"Aye," Margaret said, knowingly. "He is like ye. So too was my sister. The sight runs in our blood." She winked at Joanie.

Alec held his breath as Matthew turned and looked up at him. A jolt shot through him. The boy had one blue eye and one brown, and a scar ran down the side of his face.

"He got that when he fell off a wagon last summer." Margaret said.

Matthew held Alec's gaze without wavering. Then slowly he reached his small hand toward Alec's face and pressed his fingertip onto Alec's forehead before he closed his eyes. Alec could only wonder what the boy saw. Suddenly, Matthew's eyes flew open, and a knowing smile shaped his lips. He clasped Alec's hand and pulled him toward the door.

"Where is he taking you?" Joanie asked.

Alec lifted his shoulders. "I do not ken."

"Well, that's a first," Joanie shot back.

Alec followed the boy through the narrow village paths, passing cottages and a series of long thatch and clay huts, which he assumed housed their stores. Then the pathway opened to the village green, and on the opposite side, Alec once again saw the wooden effigy of Saint Gabriel.

Matthew dropped his hand and raced across the green and stopped in front of the angel. Alec followed and joined him. The carved saint was massive up close. Alec only came up to his chest. He stared up into the angel's face. Wooden tears coursed down his carved cheeks. Alec had never seen an angel depicted as crying, but when he looked beyond the effigy at the dozens and dozens of small wooden crosses rising out from the earth, he knew why.

"Forty-nine blessed wee souls were taken," Margaret said, coming up behind him with Joanie at her side. "I remember those dark days all too well. Two of my own are buried there.

Matthew knows. He likes to sit on my Timothy's grave. He visits him every day, some days for hours."

Alec had to fight the despair that seemed to seep from the very earth beneath his feet. Then a small, warm hand slipped into his, and he looked down into Matthew's mix-matched eyes. Immediately, clarity reclaimed his senses. "Show me," Alec said.

He followed the lad into the cemetery until he knelt in front of one of the crosses.

"That is my Timothy's grave," Margaret called.

To Alec's surprise, Matthew began tearing away at the sparse, dried bits of grass and cold earth.

"Nay, ye mustn't—" But Alec swallowed the rest of his admonishment when Matthew uncovered a piece of stone with writing carved into it. Suddenly the stone around his neck came to life as never before, searing his skin. For the first time, the heat was unbearable. He whisked the cord over his neck and glanced at his skin, which was red and blistered where the stone had lain.

Straightway, Alec dropped to his knees and helped Matthew uncover the stone. Swiping his hand across the writing, he fell back, struck to his core and stared at the words. *Alba gu bràth*.

Slowly, he straightened and leaned over the stone. Warmth caressed his face. Life pulsed around him like a beating heart. With his own heart racing, he dug his fingers into the earth, searching for the edges of the rock. It was more than three hands wide and nearly as long and thin like slate. He pried his fingers beneath it, lifting it away, revealing another stone. Alec raked both hands through his hair as he stared in amazement at a large purple stone. His eyes narrowed on the broken corner. He seized the shard from the ground and slid it into the break — a perfect fit.

Chapter Thirty

Alec closed his eyes and lay his hands on the stone and gasped as images of kings and queens and distant lands flashed in his mind's eye.

Hands shaking, he fumbled with the thin slate, covering the purple stone from sight. Then he turned to Matthew. "Ye will find some men in the tavern. One is dark haired, and two have hair as yellow as yers — one is nearly as big as Saint Gabriel," he said, gesturing to the wooden angel. "Go find them. Take them to the stables. Have them bring me a wagon."

The boy nodded and darted off.

A moment later, Joanie crouched down next to him. "What is happening?"

Alec had to tear his eyes from the ground. His heart beat harder and harder with every passing moment. He knew what he had found. Glancing back, he saw people begin to gather, watching him. "Quickly, go stand with yer Grandmother. We mustn't draw attention to what we have here. I would rather not have to answer questions from curious neighbors."

Joanie nodded. He watched her move to stand with Margaret who introduced Joanie as her granddaughter, drawing them into conversation.

Sometime later, Ramsay drove their spotted mares hitched to a rough-hewn wagon. In the back, Alec spied Nick, David, and Matthew. It wasn't until the three men hunkered down beside him that Alec dusted away the dirt he had scattered to cover the secret words of their cause.

"There's more," Alec said, meeting their stunned eyes. He slid the carved slate off, revealing the large purple stone. "We are taking this with us. It will weigh well over twenty stone. David, back the wagon as close to the fence as ye can." Then he looked at Ramsay and Nick. "We'll lift it together."

David brought the wagon as close to the site as he could without disturbing the graves while Alec, Ramsay, and Nick dug out the stone until they could fit their fingers beneath it. "Together now," Alec said. Gritting their teeth, they hoisted it out of the ground, then moved it the short distance to the wagon.

"Cover it," Alec said to David. "And guard it with yer life. This is now a mission for Scotland. Likely the most important mission we will ever carry out."

"What is it?" Ramsay pressed.

Alec locked eyes with the blacksmith. "'Tis the Stone of Destiny."

The moment the words fled his lips, a bell started to sound. He whirled around.

"What's happening?" Joanie asked.

"'Tis an alarm," Margaret gasped.

Alec felt the rider's urgency before he raced into the green. "English soldiers march this way. A band of forty strong."

"How far behind are they?" Nick called out.

"I spotted them on the road earlier this morning and took to the woods. I raced here as fast as I could. 'Tis only a matter of hours, not days."

"I wager they carry a likeness of me," Alec said under his breath to Ramsay before grabbing both Joanie and Matthew by the hands. "We're leaving," he said. Then he turned to Margaret. "Will ye come away with us?"

A glint lit her eye. "Ye just try to stop me."

Alec turned to the men. "Take the stone and Margaret to Haddington. Do not stop to rest. Change horses if ye must but make haste."

"Where will ye go?" Ramsay asked.

"We'll let them track us and head north into the mountains."

David eyes flashed bright. "Are ye planning on paying Laird Campbell a visit then?"

Alec nodded. "His Highland warriors will enjoy the extra training."

"Ye're taking the lad with ye?" Ramsay questioned. "Are ye certain that is wise?"

Alec looked down into Matthew's eyes. He could feel the boy's heart pleading to stay by his side.

"Yer destinies are somehow joined, are they not?" Margaret asked.

Alec nodded. "I believe so."

She nodded then and bent to hug Matthew close and pressed a kiss to his brow. Then she turned to Joanie. "Be strong," Margaret urged, "as ye always have been. Survive this, ye hear me?"

"I will," Joanie said firmly.

Then her grandmother pressed a kiss to her forehead and one on each cheek. "This is not goodbye, sweetling."

Chapter Thirty One

Geoffrey Mercer thundered into the village heedless of people and animals scurrying out of his path. He raced through the narrow dirt roads until he came to the village green. Behind him, the soldiers under his command fell in line, their horses dancing and snorting as they stopped short.

Geoffrey scanned the onlookers with disdain, nothing but filthy peasants, no one with any worth at all. He withdrew a scroll from his saddlebag and unrolled the large parchment. A dowel on the end weighted it down. Then he thrust his arm out, shifting in his seat to be sure everyone could see.

"I am looking for this man. My tracker believes he and his party came through here."

People turned away or gazed up at him with wide terrified eyes, but no one spoke up. Pasting a smile on his face, he called out, "Come forward. Tell me what you know, and you shall be rewarded." Then his smile disappeared, and he kicked his horse in the flank. Turning about, he grabbed the torch from the hand of his second in command. He raised the flame high. "Keep your silence, and I shall burn your stores to the ground."

Gasps and outcries arose among the growing crowd. Then a man came forward, wearing a tattered tunic and gripping a felt hat in his fingers. "I know that man," he said, his voice low.

"Speak up," Geoffrey snapped.

The man flinched. "I know that man," he said louder.

Geoffrey slid from his horse and motioned for the man to come forward. He held up the picture again of Randolph Tweed.

"Are you certain?"

Gripping tighter to his hat, his shoulders framing his ears, the man stuttered, "He ... he came through here. He had a woman with him and three other men."

"Are you certain?"

The man cast his eyes to the ground. "Aye," he said, his shoulders rising higher. "I'm sure of it."

"When they left, were they all on horseback. Did anyone walk?"

"He rode off on horseback. The others were in a wagon."

Geoffrey handed the parchment to one of his men. "Ride out," he shouted.

"Sir Knight, ye mentioned a reward."

Geoffrey scowled at the peasant. "As your reward, I will spare your life. But if you've lied to me. I will return and cut out your tongue." Then he turned his horse around and raced back the way he'd come.

The road sliced straight through a forest. Tree branches wove a tangled canopy overhead and boasted buds of spring-time, but Geoffrey did not take the time to ponder the beauty or feel the welcoming kiss of Spring's sunshine slanting through the branches. His mind remained fixed on one thing only — vengeance.

"Geoffrey," one of his guards said.

"Sir Geoffrey," he snapped. "You were there when Lord Paxton knighted me."

"Sir Geoffrey, the trail splits up ahead. A single horse headed north into the mountains. The wagon headed east. Do you want to split the men and track both?"

Geoffrey looked back at the dozens of knights on chargers behind him and smiled. He would never tire of seeing such a glorious sight. He had no intention of breaking up the men in his command. Shaking his head, he snapped at his man, "And weaken our defenses? Nay. The others are of no consequence. Only Randolph Tweed matters. Follow the rider."

JOANIE AND MATHEW PASSED the night asleep in Alec's arms while he pushed their mount ever higher. He welcomed the first light of dawn, which revealed purple mountains silhouetted against the brightening sky. Joanie and Matthew stirred, awoken by the jarring movements of their horse as the Highland landscape grew increasingly more rugged. More than once, they had to climb down and walk their mount over stretches of treacherous rocks. Still, he pushed their horse and their own stamina to maintain their lead. The English soldiers would have easily overtaken them on the open road, but their large chargers had to struggle over the same jagged rocks, steep inclines, and through the same dense woods.

Just as the sun rose overhead, a loud cry rent the air. "*Cruachan!*"

Joanie straightened, squeezing Matthew closer. "What was that?"

Her fear penetrated Alec's heart. "It was the war cry of Clan Campbell. Do not be afraid, but remain still," he warned, wrapping his arms tighter around Joanie and the wee, Matthew. "In moments, we will be surrounded."

Joanie held her breath as darting shapes streaked through the trees like racing specters in the shadows. Suddenly, men like none she had ever seen came thundering down the mountain. Their muscled bodies were clad in draping plaids that showed their sinewy bare legs. Some wore laced boots and tunics while others had bare chests and feet despite the chill in the air. Their hair hung in wild disarray well past their broad chests. In their strong hands, they gripped battle axes and swords. Some brandished small targs and others looked down at her through the hairs of their crossbows.

Behind her Alec called out words she did not understand. "*Tha mi a charaid Laird Caimbeul.*"

The warriors fell silent but kept their weapons at the ready.

"What did you say?" she whispered, her heart pounding. She fought to hold on to her courage in the presence of the wild Highlanders.

"I told them I am a friend of their lairds," he said in answer. Then he cupped his hand around his mouth and shouted. "*Alba gu bràth.*"

One man stepped forward then, a smile playing about his lips. Joanie could not help but stare at his raw masculinity. He caught her eye and dipped his head to her. She blushed, having been caught staring and lowered her gaze.

"*Cuiribh uaibh bhur buill-airm,*" the man said.

"He just told his men to lower their weapons," Alec whispered in her ear. She looked up and watched as the men sheathed their swords and lowered their axes and crossbows.

"I am Bryden Campbell, my laird's second. Who are ye?"

"Ye're both safe," Alec whispered in Joanie's ear as he swung down to the ground. "I am Alec MacVie."

Joanie watched Bryden's eyes light with recognition. "The MacVie name is well known to our clan. Alba gu bràth," he said, offering Alec his hand. Then he jerked his head up the mountain. "Ye and yer friends are welcome. I will take ye to our laird."

Alec smiled up at Matthew who stared wide-eyed at Bryden. "Aye, ye're right," Alec said, his voice low. "The Campbells are fierce warriors." Then he lifted Matthew down.

"My young cousin has a valiant heart," Joanie said as Alec helped her to the ground.

Alec turned and watched as Matthew walked straight up to Bryden.

"Blessings to ye, wee one. What is yer name?" Bryden said, hunkering down to be eye-level with the child.

"He is Matthew," Alec answered for him.

Bryden canted his head to the side, still holding Matthew's gaze. "Ye're a quiet one, are ye? Just like our laird." Bryden stood then and put a hand on Matthew's shoulder. "Just remember to speak up when it counts." Then Bryden looked back at Alec. "Come then."

When they reached the village, Alec and Laird Donnach Campbell locked eyes from across the green. Alec saw the surprise flash across the laird's features before he started toward Alec.

The Campbell's were stalwart supporters of the cause. On several occasions, Alec had run weapons and coin gathered by the Campbells down to Haddington. He and the laird had also stolen a chest of silver marks on its way to Douglas Castle, which had been seized by an English lord. Donnach was a man of great instinct and few words, which made him ideal for Alec to work with.

"I've received no word of yer coming," Donnach said simply but not unkindly when he stood in front of Alec.

"The abbot has not sent me."

He held Alec's gaze for several moments before he said, "Ye're in trouble?"

Alec nodded. "And I brought it with me and only a few hours ride behind, I'd wager."

"How many?"

"A cavalry, at least forty strong."

Slowly one side of Donnach's lips curved. Alec knew he had just whetted his appetite for battle.

Donnach cupped his hands around his lips. "*Gaisgich Rium*," he shouted. *Warriors, to me.* As the men gathered around, Alec could feel their bloodlust and passion, which poured into Alec, fueling his own lust for battle.

"I will prepare my men," Donnach said, turning once more to Alec. "Take yer woman and the lad to the keep. Eat and rest. We will take position in the mountains in one hour.

Chapter Thirty Two

Joanie sat at a crowded trestle table with Matthew at her side within the great room of Dunnoch's keep. Highland women, children, and older men filled the tables and the room nigh to bursting, all waiting to send their men off to battle. Joanie had felt her life threatened often enough to understand the tension building in the room, but she knew nothing of warfare. Still, she forced her nerves to quiet. She did not wish to make Matthew anxious, although as she looked into his uncanny eyes, she knew that like Alec, he probably already felt what she tried to conceal.

The door to the great hall opened, drawing her gaze to where one of the warriors stood and called everyone to the bailey. Joanie held tightly to Matthew's hand as they joined the others filing into the yard. The late afternoon sun cast cool shadows across the faces of the warriors, who stood in rows in front of Laird Campbell. Like Bryden and the other Highland warriors, Dunnoch was impressive to behold with his thick, corded muscles and long, tangled brown hair.

She scanned the men, looking for Alec but did not see him at first. Then her breath caught. Alec came forward and took his place next to Bryden. He was dressed like the other Highland warriors in a plaid with naught else but leather boots. In one hand, he gripped a targ and as usual, his sword was strapped to his back. He looked tall and lean next to the Campbell warriors, none of whom reached Alec in height. His black eyes gleamed, harder and more intense than ever. He motioned for her to come to him. Leading Matthew behind her, she did as he bade.

His black eyes bore into her soul. Handing his targ to Matthew to hold, he cupped her cheeks and kissed her, slowly, a lingering kiss that filled her core with honeyed warmth and stirred a longing within her that grew and grew. She clung to him, returning his kiss with all her love, all her passion. When he drew away, he did not speak. The pulse of his body flowed through her, conveying his every intent and thought. *I love you, body and soul.*

A rush of tears flooded her eyes. "I love you too," she whispered, reaching her arms high. Knowing what she wanted, he lifted her feet off the ground, pulling her close, and she buried her face in his neck, inhaling his masculine scent.

Feeling her fear for his safety, he spoke softly to her. "The men around me are not afraid. Ye ken I would feel it if they were. Forty cavalry on an open battlefield would mean risk, but still I do not doubt the Campbell warriors would come out the winners. But here, on their mountain — this isn't battle. 'Tis target practice." Fear continued to grip her heart. He set her on her feet, and once more he cupped her cheeks. "Do ye think I would have led English soldiers here if I thought I would be placing these good men in danger? Look around ye, Joanie," he said, dropping his hands to his sides. "Go ahead," he urged her. "Look."

She took a deep breath and slowly considered the warriors who smiled down at their women or kissed them lovingly. Others held their own sweet children in their arms.

"You know how this all ends, then?"

"I feel in my heart that something wondrous is about to happen, but I do not ken what. What I do know, as plain and true as my love for ye, is that every man ye see here will return this day to their families."

"Including you," she whispered. It felt as if a boulder crushed her chest, forcing her to draw shallow breaths.

"Including me," he said, pulling her against him. "Just keep breathing. I will return." His lips claimed hers. This time his kiss was hungry, demanding. It dissolved the weight on her chest, opening her heart to his promise of victory.

"I love ye, Joanie," he said. Her knees grew weak at the sight of his smile. Then he crouched low, and she watched as he looked at Matthew. They were a sight to see with Alec's intense black gaze and Matthew's uncanny mix-matched eyes. They needed no words to convey what was in their hearts and minds. Her heart flooded with warmth when Matthew wrapped his arms around Alec's neck. A smile full of life's wonder teased Alec's lips as he returned the child's hug. Then he stood and stepped back in line with the other men the instant before Dunnoch raised his sword in the air and shouted, "*Cruachan.*"

"Breathe," he said again, his fiery eyes locked with hers. Then his face settled into cold, hard lines as the battle cry tore from his lips. Turning away from her, he joined the other warriors as they stormed through the gate, their strides long and powerful.

She wrapped her arms around herself, feeling the absence of Alec's touch and stared after him, her eyes lingering on his sleek form long after it had disappeared. Remembering his last word to her, she drew a deep breath and turned to take

Matthew's hand to lead him back into the keep, but he was gone.

She scanned the courtyard for him. "Matthew," she called.

Spying the stables, she dashed across the courtyard, thinking he might have wanted to see the horses. She peered into every stall before she rushed back outside.

Panic building in her heart, she grabbed a woman who was passing by. "Have you seen the small boy who arrived with me today. His name is Matthew."

"The one with the strange eyes?" she asked.

"Yes," Joanie exclaimed, daring to hope.

But the women shook her head.

Another woman nearby called out to her. "I saw him run off with the other lads. They've gone to watch the battle from the cliffs."

Joanie's eyes widened with alarm. Then she turned and started to race toward the gate.

"Wait," the woman cried. "Ye can't go out there like that." She swept the plaid from her shoulders and wrapped it around Joanie's. "Ye don't need to do this. The lads will be all right."

"I cannot let anything happen to him. He's my family. He's…" Her words trailed off, blocked by the knot lodged in her throat.

"There, there, pet. I can see ye're not to be swayed," she said. Then she untied a sheathed dirk from her waist and tied it to Joanie's. "Don't get too close to the battle and mind the cliffs. 'Tis still icy on the rocks."

Chapter Thirty Three

Alec could hear his heart thunder in his chest along with the hearts of the men scattered in the mountain around him. The din pulsed like a battle march in his mind, ever fueling his lust for justice. Every man kept his eyes trained on the narrow pass below for the first light glinting off the knights' helmets, but not Alec. He saw in ways others could not. He closed his eyes and opened his heart and mind and waited for the first taste of the knights' anger and frustration as they tried to pull their hulking chargers up the steep mountainside.

At first, their souls grazed his, a trickle of weary aggression that grew with every step they climbed. Then the hearts of the Highland warriors scattered around him began to race harder, and he knew without opening his eyes that the first glint of sunshine on metal had been spotted. Almost there, he breathed, his eyes still closed. Slowly, he reached back and gripped the hilt of his sword. He could feel the blood rushing faster through his body, awakening his limbs in anticipation of the Campbell war cry. "Now," he said out loud the instant before Dunnoch sounded the call.

Violent fury shot threw Alec as he threw his head back and bellowed the word, joining the roar that echoed down the mountain. An instant later, the fear of the men below struck his heart. Pure terror raged within him — but it was not his fear. Nor did it belong to his fellow warriors. The enemy's hearts quaked as they beheld the half-naked, fierce warriors pouring down the pass and leaping at them from the rocks above with teeth bared, like Hell raining down upon their unwitting souls, souls who hadn't seen the attack coming.

JOANIE CONTINUED TO breathe, holding fast to her courage as she followed the gruesome sounds of battle. The wild calls of the warriors fed her valor while the strangled screams of the dying knights struck her heart. She shuddered at the thought of Matthew hearing those same cries. The mountain was no place for a child. She only peeked down at the tangled chaos of limbs and swords for a moment before she turned to look up and scan the ridge above. At last, she spotted the boys staring down at the swinging swords and the bloodshed below. Then she saw him. "Matthew," she gasped before she scurried up the mountainside.

FURY AND FEAR BATTLED for domination over Geoffrey's mind as he watched the fray from a short distance away. A nagging apprehension had pricked at his mind as they had climbed higher up the rocky pass, and so he had moved to the back of the line. He could always count on his instincts being right. He seethed with rage as he watched Randolph Tweed, wearing the savage garb of the Highlander, strike down his men. Surrounded and massively outnumbered, his men fell one after the other. He gaped in horror as a wild Highlander jumped from a boulder jutting out from the mountain side, cleaving Geoffrey's accomplished tracker's head from his body. Blasted savages! His heart pounded in his ears. He had no choice but to retreat farther down the mountain while his body was still intact. He backed a few steps down, and just as he was about to turn and run, he froze. Tendrils of long, unbound black hair lifted in the breeze, like fingers beckoning him upward. His servant, his rightful property, his Joanie scrambled up the slope beyond the reach of the fray.

He gritted his teeth at the sight of her. He might have lost the battle. His soldiers were being slaughtered before his very eyes, but he could not allow her to win. Giving the battle a wide berth, he headed up the slope after her.

He climbed ever higher, his progress slowed by the slick ice that shone in the soft light of the setting sun. He rounded a steep slope, reaching the cliffs where he spied Joanie and several boys peering down at the battle. Greed pushing him faster, he slipped and landed with a thud, drawing their gazes.

He saw her, and she gasped, yanking a small boy to his feet and backing farther up the jagged cliff. The other boys climbed down the rocks. Then, with practiced ease, they shimmied across the ledge to the opposite slope. He trained his gaze higher, not interested in the Highland whelps. He wanted one thing only — the bitch with the haunting voice whose meddling had set his defeat in motion.

He scampered up the slope, but again his foot slipped on a patch of ice and he fell, landing hard on his shoulder.

"Blast you," he shouted. Finding his footing once more, he rounded a tall, jutting rock and saw her. A jolt of victory surged through him. She had reached the final precipice. There was no more mountain to climb.

"Stay back," she cried, clutching the boy to her side.

Geoffrey leered at her. "I will do whatever I want," he spat. "You belong to me." He lunged for her, but she slashed at him with a dagger she had hidden behind her back.

"I am not afraid of you," she cried, standing strong, dagger at the ready. "Not anymore."

He gritted his teeth at her. "You are going to beg for death before I'm through with you." He unsheathed his blade and stepped toward her, but then a blinding light erupted behind her. He cried out, shielding his eyes.

Peering through his fingers, he stared in awe at radiant beams, so clean and pure that it burned his dark soul to gaze upon them, and yet he could not tear his eyes away. He shuddered as fear like none he had ever known before gripped his quaking heart. The light softened and shimmered and gave way to a figure dressed all in white. Her flaxen hair gleamed. Her skin sparkled like diamonds, and her eyes burned with green fire. He knew her face.

"Do not look at me," he cried. His legs gave way. He collapsed to the ground the instant before he glimpsed the flicker of wings. Then arms, ethereal and translucent, encircled Joanie from behind. He couldn't speak or move or breathe. Then the boy stepped forward with eyes that stripped Geoffrey bare. "Ye will never hurt anyone again," the boy said, his voice echoing like thunder in Geoffrey's mind. "Now it is yers to bear."

Geoffrey bellowed, his mouth straining wide as waves of pain and shame shot through him. He fought to stand as he absorbed every hurt he had ever inflicted on those he should have protected. Staggering away from his own sins, his foot slipped on the ice. For a moment, he felt suspended in air before another wave of pain battered his soul, and the world fell away as he plummeted off the cliff, the brightly colored lights receding into darkness.

Breathless, Joanie stared in disbelief at the place where Geoffrey had stood only moments before, cowering. Her heart pounded. She couldn't believe what had just happened. Her hands gripped her head as she struggled to understand. Then she looked down at Matthew and bent low, hugging him close. "It was you, wasn't it?" She pulled away and looked into his powerful eyes. "You did this. You found your words and frightened him."

Matthew shook his head. "She gave them to me."

Confused, Joanie scanned the cliffs. "Who did? There is no one here but you and me."

Matthew smiled. "And Diana."

Joanie sucked in a sharp breath. "What did you just say?"

He looked at the empty space to her left. "She is standing there, beside ye."

Trembling, Joanie slowly stood. "I ... I cannot see her."

"That doesn't mean she isn't there."

Tears stung Joanie's eyes as she swept her trembling hand through the air beside her.

"She says it was her turn to protect ye."

Joanie's hand clamped on her mouth as a sob racked her shoulders.

"She says she loves ye."

"I love you, Diana," Joanie blurted out through her tears. "I love you so much."

And then a silken breeze swirled around her, encircling her in warmth that penetrated her heart, her very soul. And she knew then that her dearest friend, her sister in life, lived on, forever young, forever beautiful. And never again would Joanie doubt the power of angels.

ALEC SURGED UP THE mountain driven by Joanie's fear, which coursed through his body, darkening his soul. The blood of the enemy stained his hands, and yet he knew one English knight had escaped and threatened the woman he loved, the woman he would steal for, fight for, die for. He squeezed the hilt of his sword and narrowed his eyes on the path, dodging ice and hurdling rocks. When he crested the summit, he stopped short as pure wonder seized his heart, lifting him from the darkness and bloodshed into beauty without compare. He dropped to his knees. An ethereal Diana, encircled Joanie in beams of heavenly light, filling her, loving her, healing her.

Joanie's serenity and her replete heart brought tears to his eyes. Through the watery blur, he watched Diana's glory dissolve into myriad points of light that hovered above their heads for only a moment, a breath before soaring high, filling the newly twilight sky with flickering stars.

Matthew reached him first, a breath before Joanie. Alec pulled them both into his arms.

"Did ye see her?" Matthew exclaimed, his face shining up at him.

Alec's eyes widened at the sound of Matthew's voice, and his heart, which he never would have believed could be any fuller, nigh burst from his chest. He smiled into Matthew's mix-matched eyes. "I did."

Joanie beamed up at him, her eyes brighter than he had ever seen them.

"Then we were both wrong," she said. "Angels do exist."

A smile tugged at one side of his lips as he leaned down to press his forehead to hers. "Aye, we were both wrong, but only about angels. Everything else about us is just right."

Epilogue

Haddington Abbey, Scotland

Three days later

A twinkle filled Abbot Matthew's eyes. "Ye ken what this is?" he asked, removing the green silk cloth that covered the stone.

"I do," Alec said.

He, Joanie, and Matthew had followed the abbot deep in the abbey cellars. Torch fire danced on the stone walls and illuminated the large stone.

"When Ramsay and David arrived with the Stone, I admit I was more than surprised." He turned and put his hand on Alec's shoulder. "I shouldn't have been, though."

"I was more than a little surprised myself," Alec said. "I thought King Edward seized the Stone. In fact, I've heard it said that he built a throne around it. He sits on it even now in York."

"Thanks to the brothers at Glenrose Abbey, the Stone of Destiny is by no means under the posterior of that wretched king."

Brows drawn, Alec said, "I saw flashes of Templar knights attacking the abbey. Did the monks switch the stones when they saw the soldiers approach?"

"Nay, the stone that had been displayed near the altar was never the true stone. It had been hidden away somewhere either in the abbey itself or within the grounds; only the monks knew. After the king raided the abbey in 1296 and stole the fake stone, the monks relocated the true stone away from Glenrose. They managed as well as they could during the move, but they dropped it and a shard broke off. They later gave the shard to the Bishop Lamberton as proof that Edward had been fooled. Still, they did not even tell the bishop of the Stone's whereabouts. Then, just two years later, Edward sacked the abbey again, which meant he must have suspected what happened. Of course, nothing came of the raid. The bishop was still assured that the real stone remained in Scotland.

"But then the brothers disappeared," Alec said, knowingly.

The abbot nodded gravely and made the sign of the cross. "May God protect them and keep them safe. Aye, and disappearing with them was the Stone's secret location. That was when the bishop came to me and told me all he knew." He held up the shard. "He charged me with finding the Stone, but all I had to go on was this." Then he rested his hand on Alec's shoulder. "And yer seeing eyes."

"Forgive me, Abbot," Joanie said, "but I still do not understand why the Stone warmed in my presence, and how it led us to Saint Gabriel. How did we find it?"

The abbot smiled. "I am but a simple man, Joanie. There is little I can reveal that ye do not already know. But what I can tell ye is that I don't believe ye found the Stone."

Her brows pinched together. "But you said this was, indeed, the true stone."

"What I mean to say is that I believe the Stone found ye. Ye see, Joanie, the Stone of Destiny is as old as time itself." The abbot placed his hand reverently on the purple rock. "It holds the breath of the Holy Spirit. The power it contains cannot be understood by any of us."

"Why then do you think it chose us?" she asked.

"The stone remained hidden in that grave for more than five years. People passed it again and again, but its pleas fell on deaf hearts — hearts without the capacity to truly hear." The abbot turned. "Then ye three came along."

Alec rubbed the back of his neck. "But I held that shard for months and saw nothing."

The abbot raised a brow at Alec. "And in all that time, ye maintained walls around your heart and mind. Now, if I had to venture a guess, I don't believe Joanie's presence truly made the stone warm, I think she warmed yer heart, allowing ye to let down yer shields."

"Still, how did the Stone know that Joanie and Matthew were connected."

"So many questions, but Alec, where is yer faith? Did ye ever think that maybe, it was just destiny?"

Alec paused, then wrapped his arm around Joanie's waist and clasped Matthew close. "That I can believe."

The abbot swept the fabric back in place. "The Stone's journey is not yet done, for it cannot stay here. It must be hidden away again." Then he turned back and looked at Alec. "Ye too must be hidden away. Yer a wanted man now. So, ye ken what that means."

Alec smiled. "We journey to Colonsay to join my outlaw brothers."

SPRING'S FULL WARMTH caressed Joanie's face as she looked up at the crisp blue sky crowded with gulls soaring high. She watched as one broke away, diving headlong into the water, emerging a second later, victorious with a small fish in its beak.

Mathew stirred. She looked down where he slept, his head rested in her lap.

"It does my old heart good to see that lad so happy," Margaret said from where she sat at the bow. "He needed a family of his own."

Alec smiled as he adjusted the sail. "His family is about to grow significantly." Then he pointed toward a wide, crescent shaped shore. "Colonsay!"

Alec's father first hailed from Colonsay before he journeyed to the once bustling city of Berwick to work the docks. When his brother, Jack, had to go on the run, escaping the wrath of King Edward with English lady, Bella Ravensworth, and her father at his side, he chose to hideaway at Colonsay, knowing the MacVies would always be welcome.

Alec knew in his heart that Jack had made it, outrunning Edward's men. His youngest brother, Ian, followed after to Colonsay, escorting their sister, Rose, and Jack's lassies — wee orphans Jack had adopted after their parents were slaughtered during the massacre. Whether Quinn or Rory had made it to Colonsay, he did not know, but that would soon change.

The keel of their small boat carved into the golden sand. Alec leapt into the crashing waves and pulled the boat free from the consuming force of the sea. Then he reached up and aided first Matthew, then Margaret, and finally, Joanie down to the shore, although he held Joanie close and breathed in the salty scent of her hair before he set her toes on the soft sand.

He scanned the shore. There was a long pier with two moorings that jutted out into the waves. Small sailboats hugged the pier, rhythmically bumping into the wood with every wave that lapped toward shore. A shift in the direction of the wind, sparked a feeling in his heart.

"Wait for me here," he said to Joanie. Then he set out down the curved shore.

Beyond a tall jetty of rocks, he spotted a woman, tall and slim, with wild red curls that tumbled to her waist. His sister, Rose, stood with a shawl loosely draped about her shoulders as she gazed out at the choppy waves.

When Rose was a little girl, she dreamt that love would come to her from the sea, and she used to stand for hours at the docks, watching, waiting.

"Just as I always remember ye, staring out to sea."

Rose gasped when she turned and locked eyes with Alec. Instantly, she started toward him, but then she froze. "Ye're nothing like how I remembered ye."

She walked up to him tentatively, curiously studying his face. When he smiled, she jumped a little, and her hand flew to cover her mouth. "Alec MacVie, what has come over ye?"

Still smiling, he shrugged. "I'm happy."

Her brow's pinched together. "Ye're happy?"

He laughed and seized her by the waist, lifting her and swirling her about. "Aye, my dear, big sister, I'm happy."

Rose wrapped her arms around his neck. When she pulled away, her blue eyes shone bright, brimming with tears.

She swiped the few drops that had escaped. "Well, all right, then, Alec, don't make me wait any longer. I would like to thank the woman who has made my little brother so very happy."

Alec took Rose by the hand and led her back around to the sandy beach and introduced Rose to his new family.

Rose gently cupped Joanie's cheeks, her lips pressed in a thin line, forcing back her tears. "Oh, aye, ye and Alec are one and the same. I can tell." Then she turned back to Alec. "Wait until the lads see ye."

"Where have they built their homes?" Alec asked.

"Just beyond that ridge," Rose said.

The shore rose up from the grabbing waves. Then golden sand gave way to tall sea grass, which hugged the base of some short cliffs.

Alec turned to Matthew. "Do ye want to run ahead and announce our arrival?"

Matthew smiled and nodded. "How will I know them?"

"Ye'll know. MacVie men are hard to miss."

Matthew darted across the sea grass and scrambled up the cliffs.

"Don't think for a moment that I can make it up those cliffs," Margaret said.

Rose laughed. "Not to worry. There's some stairs carved into the stone, over on the left side."

Joanie took Margaret's hand and helped her into the tall grasses while Alec encircled Joanie's waist with his arm.

"And there they are," Rose said, pointing.

A large, powerful looking man with broad shoulders and curly black hair appeared. Even from the distance, Joanie could appreciate his raw masculinity with his chiseled jaw and deep-set eyes. On his arm was a woman with long sable brown hair and beautiful olive skin.

"That is Jack, the eldest of my brothers with his Bella on his arm," Alec said.

Then another couple appeared. The man had long wavy black hair. He was tall and broad, although less so than Jack but still brawnier than Alec and ruggedly handsome. Joanie could see that there were, indeed, common traits enjoyed by the MacVie men. Ebony hair, full lips, deep-set eyes. She guessed their eyes were every bit as dark as Alec's. Joanie had to tear her gaze away from the man to consider the woman at his side. Like Bella, she had rich olive skin, but her hair was every bit as black as the men's.

"That is Quinn. He was born just after Jack. As for the lovely woman on his arm, I have no idea who she is," Alec said.

Rose smiled. "She is Catarina, Bella's sister."

"Bella's sister?" Alec exclaimed. "That's a story I can't wait to hear. Och, there's Rory!"

Joanie gasped as she watched Alec's younger brother jump the height of two men from the ridge of the cliff to the sand below.

"Aye, that's Rory, all right, the second most reckless person ye are likely to meet," Rose said. "And here comes his Alex, the most reckless of all."

Joanie gasped as a woman with long blond hair, not unlike Diana's, jumped the same height, landing in Rory's arms. Then Rory put her on her feet, and they both started racing toward them.

Rose laughed. "They just wanted to be the first to greet ye."

But no sooner did Rory start his sprint, then the other MacVie men joined the race. But all three stopped short when they drew close enough to see into Alec's eyes. Joanie watched as all three brothers stared, expressions of curious wonderment etched on their handsome faces. Then, in two strides, Jack closed the distance between them and pulled Alec into a fierce hug. Joanie's heart flooded with warmth when Alec returned Jack's hug with the same force. Then in a flash of black hair,

Quinn and Rory joined the embrace in a tangle of strong arms and the same fierce affection.

"Wait for me," a deep baritone voice shouted.

Joanie whirled around and saw a giant fireball disguised as a man hurtling toward them with Matthew bouncing impossibly high up on his massive shoulders. Ian was exactly as Helena had described, right down to the long, flaming red hair. He smiled at Joanie when he passed by, his blue eyes as bright as the summer sky and his face so warm and kind that she felt like she was looking at the sun — but a gentle, steadfast sun that would never go away and leave someone in the dark.

"Hold tight, my wee man," he said to Matthew. Then he stretched his arms wide. "Here I come," Ian bellowed to his brothers.

"Oh, go on then," Rose laughed and joined her brothers with arms spread wide.

LATER THAT EVENING, Alec stood on the cliffs with Joanie at his side. The last sliver of sunlight shimmered on the horizon, casting jewel colored light across the sky and waves.

"I never could have imagined a place as beautiful as Colonsay or a family as big and full of love. I only wish..." her voice trailed off as her gaze shifted beyond the shore to the jetty where Rose stood, gazing out at sea. "I know she is quick to laugh, and her smile never falters, but..." She turned and looked up at Alec. "Her heart is so very sad, isn't it?"

A soft smiled curved Alec's lips. "Aye, she is, but fear not." A twinkle glinted in his eye, like a lone star in the night sky. "One day, her true love will wash up on shore."

Joanie smiled and threw her arms around his neck. "I believe you, and I love you." Then she looked into his seer's eyes. "Thank you for saving my life."

He crushed her against him and kissed her just as the sun dipped from sight and twilight encircled them in soft hues of gray and violet. Then he pulled away slightly and whispered. "Thank ye for saving mine."

The End

Thank you for reading Alec: A Scottish Outlaw. What's next?

Keep reading to find out!

ROSE: A SCOTTISH OUTLAW
What people are saying...

"This book was absolutely perfect."
"Love! Love! Love!"
"Heartfelt and brilliantly written."
"The best of the series!"

An excerpt from Rose: A Scottish Outlaw
COLONSAY, SCOTLAND 1303

Rose MacVie stood on her favorite rock, gazing at the moon, which hovered above the twilight-blue sea. It cast a rippling white reflection, stretching like an arm across the water.

The moon reached for Rose.

She felt the pull within her, the light straining to touch her lonely, restless heart—for the moon was a kindred spirit. It, too, knew what it meant to be alone. Fire blazed inside the heavenly body that could never be fully released. It hung in the night sky, cool and somber, with only the softest light able to escape the confines of its celestial skin.

Like the moon, Rose could never escape her fate. Fire forever burned inside her. Some days it blazed red-hot, cruelly licking the open wounds in her heart—three deep, cavernous, and bloody gashes that could never heal, not in a thousand years, not in this world or the next.

"Ye've been out here for a long time."

Rose whirled around. Ian, her youngest brother, stood behind her, a gentle smile curving his lips.

"I've been waiting for ye on the beach for hours now," he said, his voice kind. He moved toward her tentatively as if she were an animal he did not wish to spook. "I have something for ye."

Rose turned back to face the water and drew a deep breath, fighting to suppress the pit of emptiness that threatened to consume her from the inside out. She had to be strong. Ian needed her. Once more, swallowing her own pain, she silently bid goodnight to the moon and the sea.

They would be there for her again as sure as her need for them would return.

Joining Ian, they walked the shore together in silence for several minutes. At length, he said, "Ye haven't been at supper for a few nights." His tone held a casualness she knew he did not feel.

Despite how he tried, Ian could not hide his concern for her, none of her brothers could. But they did not worry alone. Having felt listless for months and months, she fretted over her own wellbeing. But what her brothers didn't know was how lonely their nightly suppers made her feel.

Jack, Quinn, and Rory were all happily married now with children of their own. And just last week, Alec and Joanie announced they were going to have a baby. In her heart, Rose could not have been happier for them. Alec and Joanie were no strangers to suffering. They had to walk through hell and back to find the happiness that now shaped their lives. But somehow the fullness of their love made the emptiness of her own arms that much clearer.

Rose scowled—not at Ian or Alec or any of her brothers. The person she scorned was herself. Why must she despair? Where had her spirit gone?

She knew the answer.

Despite how happy she was for her siblings, she could not help but feel peripheral to their life on the island. Her family's lives continued to evolve while hers remained the same—no different now than after that tragic day eight years ago when her own family had been taken from her.

Once upon a time, the MacVies had lived ordinary lives as fishermen and dockhands within the heart of Berwick, Scotland's busiest and most prosperous port. But the hammer of Longshanks—the English King—pummeled the city to nothing. When the dust settled, thousands of innocents had been slaughtered, including her husband and their three precious daughters.

In the beginning, there had been only anguish, blinding pain that stole her breath, her mind, her soul, even her will to live. She never would have made it through those dark days following the massacre if her brothers hadn't needed her.

Years later, the grief still flowed through her. It lived in her blood, in the food she tasted, and in the flowers she smelled. It was ubiquitous as the stars at night or the sea that stretched for all eternity. But she had made peace with her pain. She did not rail against it anymore, nor did she try to ignore it. It was a part of her, no different than her hands or her feet or the heart that beat in her chest.

But something darker than grief had begun to move within her, something insidious and consuming—an emptiness that left her always tired and so very lonely. It mocked her and judged her, making her feel unworthy of happiness.

She dug in her heels, stopping in her tracks.

She pressed her hand over her mouth, silencing the sob that ached to be freed. She couldn't draw breath as, once more, her mind's eye revealed the monotony of her own life stretching out before her, empty and unchanging, year after year dragging to a close without the warmth of a man lying beside her or her children to care for or grandchildren to bounce on her knee.

Brows drawn, Ian reached for her. "What is it?" he asked.

Tears stung her eyes. She stepped free from his embrace. "I'm sorry, Ian. I don't know what's wrong with me."

"Aye, ye do," he said, his tone gentle but insistent. "Ye just don't want to say it, because ye hate to complain. But I'm giving ye permission. Right now, Rose, say what ye feel."

She clenched her fists, her heart unraveling beyond the confines of her usual control. "I just want more for myself." She opened her hands, palms up. "They're so empty when once they were so very full." She dropped her hands to her side. "I may have many years left to my life. I do not want to spend them steeped in naught but regret."

Once again, Ian pulled her close. "Ye ken ye're not truly alone. Ye will always have yer family."

She pressed her lips tight against the familiar platitude. "Ye must think me so ungrateful," she said through clenched teeth, angry at her own weakness.

Ian crooked his thumb beneath her chin, forcing her to meet his gaze. "I didn't mean to diminish yer words. I just need to affirm to ye how essential and loved ye are. But of us all, 'tis ye who has suffered most, and ye're more than entitled to yer feelings." He shook his head. "I wish there was some way I could take it all away. If I could reach up to heaven and pluck yer daughters from the sky, I would."

Rose's shoulders sagged. She took a deep breath. "No one can. And although I grieve for them every day, a part of me understands this and has reconciled myself to my fate—But 'tis my fate that mocks me with its barrenness." She stretched her arms wide as if to encompass the whole of Colonsay. "And this island. This wonderful haven that protects all I hold dear, my heroic brothers who have sacrificed their freedom for Scotland—who are outlaws to the crown, wanted men. This island has saved them, allowed them a place where they can live happily ever after. But this is a place to end up, not to begin. I will never find what my heart craves on these isolated shores."

Ian seized her hands, his eyes bright with hope. "But don't ye see, this is just the beginning for the MacVies—a new beginning. I'm going to make us merchants. We will have ships, Rose, big ones." He pulled her farther down the coast and stopped in front of a large bulky object, completely covered by an old, patched sail cloth. He turned to her. "And I'll need a quarter master."

She pressed her hand to her chest. "Me?" she said, not hiding her surprise. Then she cocked her brow at her youngest brother. "Ian, no man in his right mind will sail a ship with a woman as its quarter master."

Ian puffed out his chest. Although he was only one and twenty, he stood more than six and a half feet tall. With his fiery red curls, he was an intimidating sight. A gentle pup, more often than not, but when provoked, he had an explosive temper. So, too, had she in her youth, but over the years she had learned control...most of the time, at least.

He crossed his arms over his massive chest. "They will if they want to sail my ship." With his next breath, he relaxed and smiled. The lion once more gave way to the lamb. "Anyway," he continued, "ye're a fine sailor. Ye always bring us luck when ye join us fishing. And speaking of fishing..." he said, a smile spreading across his face as he reached for the large sail cloth that covered whatever he sought to conceal. "This is for ye." He whisked the cloth away.

She gasped, and a smile came unbidden to her lips while her gaze traced the sleek lines of a newly fashioned sailing skiff. Although large enough for two passengers, she was certain she could handle the small vessel on her own. Jumping high, she threw her arms around Ian's neck. "'Tis magnificent!"

He laughed and squeezed her tightly before setting her feet back on the ground.

Her hand shook as she ran her fingers across the oarlock. "I've never seen anything so beautiful." Still smiling, she looked up at Ian. "Will ye try her out with me on the morrow?"

His smile faltered, causing her own to disappear. "What is it?" she asked.

He looked at her for a moment as if measuring his words.

"Just say whatever is on yer mind. Ye know I do not suffer such nonsense as sparing my feelings. What is it?"

He set his lips in a grim line before saying, "I received a missive from Abbot Matthew earlier today."

A chill of dread shot up her spine. "I...I did not know a messenger came," she stammered while she fought for calm.

Ian rubbed the back of his neck. "Ye've stayed away. No one wanted to disturb ye."

Abbot Matthew led Scotland's army of secret rebels. Jack, Quinn, Rory, and Alec had all carried out missions for the abbot, but they had retired their swords, all except Ian. She knew there was only one reason why the abbot would have sent a message to her youngest brother. The cause for Scottish independence needed a MacVie, and Ian was the only one left whose identity remained a secret.

"Ye're wanted for a mission," she said quietly.

he nodded. "I leave at daybreak."

She turned away and looked out to sea, her heartache both soothed and fueled by the tumultuous waves.

"Rose," he said.

"Aye," she muttered. Her chest felt hollow as if her heart was too empty to beat.

"Abbot Matthew once told me that God is like the stars guiding a man's ship, but 'tis the man who makes his own destiny." He wrapped his arm around her shoulders and started to lead her up the beach toward the large, thatched hut where the MacVies had gathered to give Ian a send-off.

"What are ye trying to tell me?" she asked.

"I'm telling ye that yer destiny is not yet written."

TRISTAN THATCHER ONCE again read the saccharine words scratched by his father's hand on the rumpled missive delivered that morning when his ship pulled into Port Rìgh on Skye.

Dear Tristan,

I have the most joyous news to share with you, my son.

"Joyous, indeed," Tristan muttered angrily, his brow furrowing deeper still.

With regard to procuring for you a wife, I have made the most propitious match.

"Favorable for all involved accept me," he scoffed and lunged to his feet, continuing to read.

Prepare yourself, my son, for good tidings.

Tristan skimmed through the next several paragraphs summarizing Baron Roxwell's poorly managed estates and dwindling coffers, for which Tristan's father could not be more delighted—the reason for his glee was where Tristan started to read more closely.

Baron Roxwell's daughter, Abigail, is a comely enough lass.

"What does it matter when her heart's as black as soot," he snapped angrily at the parchment, which refused to satisfy his temper with a reply he could shoot down. Resisting the urge to crumple the already abused paper in his fist, he read on.

Baron Roxwell has consented to a betrothal between you and Abigail. Thus, uniting our families and making you Lord Tristan Thatcher. It is a dream come true.

A sharp rapping sounded at the door the instant before it swung open and a tall, slender man entered Tristan's cramped quarters.

"This is a nightmare, but one from which I cannot wake," Tristan growled to his quarter master.

Philip leaned against the door. "Can I assume you have not figured a way out of your betrothal?"

Tristan held up the parchment. "I have read my father's letter countless times, hoping I somehow missed the jest."

Philip shook his head. "I believe your father is gravely serious. Unfortunately for you, he means every word. I'm sorry, Captain, but you're as good as married."

Tristan sat down at his small desk, determined to read the letter again. "We must have missed something. My father cannot mean to have betrothed me without my consent—while I'm leagues away. I am five and thirty. Fathers do not betroth their grown sons."

He had no wish to disrespect his father, but he also refused to be a pawn in Owen Thatcher's pursuit of something that was contrary to Tristan's beliefs. It was not marriage itself that he opposed, although as a sailor he never fancied the idea of marrying a woman only to leave her alone most of the year. It was his father's desire for an aristocratic title that Tristan fundamentally opposed.

He had never understood his father's fascination with the peerage. Tristan saw the lot as lazy and entitled leeches who thrived off the labor of others. Unlike the Thatcher family, Baron Roxwell had not earned his esteemed position in society. He had simply been born to it. In contrast, Tristan's father had started out a penniless London dockhand. Over the years, Owen worked his way to Captain. And when Tristan came of age, he had propelled the family business forward. Now, they were some of the most successful merchants in Christendom with fleets of ships that traveled from the North Sea to the Mediterranean. Still, somehow this wasn't enough for Owen.

Another knock sounded. "Enter," he barked.

A thin, freckled face slowly peered around the door. "Sorry, Captain. I didn't mean to intrude."

Tristan took a deep breath. He could tell his brash tone had startled his cabin boy. "You needn't apologize, Simon." He held up the letter in his hand. "A matter of grave importance has vexed me, but it is my problem, not yours. What do you have to report?"

A smile replaced Simon's frown. "Nelson has spotted something drifting toward us."

Tristan dropped the letter on his narrow bed. "Let us go see what he has found."

Both Simon and Philip backed into the hallway, allowing Tristan to take lead up the stairs. Stepping onto the main deck, Tristan scanned his ship. His crew lined the starboard side, clearly struggling to see what Nelson had spotted from his high perch.

Tristan cupped his hands around his mouth. "What do you see, Nelson?"

A thin, grizzly face with a nearly toothless grin smiled down at him over the sides of the crow's nest, but, an instant later, his smile vanished as the line he held slipped from his gnarled fingers. Quickly, Nelson scampered from his perch and nimbly crossed the yard, seizing the line before he climbed back into the lookout. Tristan grinned up at the ancient sailor whose wiry body moved like a man a quarter of his age.

Again, the weathered face peered down from above. "Can't say for certain yet, Captain, but there's something adrift out there." Then he pointed up to the twilight-blue sky. "'Tis a blessing it be summer, and the moon is full. Whatever sails this way will not be able to sneak up on us. I'll see it first."

"Good man," Tristan called. "Keep your eyes starboard. I wait for your report."

"Aye aye, Captain."

Tristan crossed the main deck and climbed the stairs to the forecastle and was soon joined by Philip. Keeping his eyes trained on the shadowy sea, Tristan said to his quarter master, "I must find a way out of this betrothal without shaming my father."

"Shaming him?" Philip said, the incredulity in his tone drew Tristian's gaze. "Captain, if you refuse this betrothal, your father could be thrown in the stocks or imprisoned. By the Saints, you speak of breaking a contract with nobility. His very life may be forfeit and yours."

Tristan gripped the ship's rail, releasing a frustrated growl. "There must be a way. You know Baron Roxwell's character. He's a deplorable man. His own gambling and greed have brought his family low enough that he would consider betrothing his daughter to a commoner."

Philip arched his brow at him. "You may not be of noble birth, but I would hardly call you common. You are wealthier than many lords."

Tristan threw his hands up. "What does it matter? I refuse to bind myself to such a ruthless family. Baron Roxwell is the epitome of all I despise in their class."

Philip looked at him dead on. "I'm sorry, Captain. The only way this match might have been avoided is if you were already married when the message arrived."

Tristan fisted his hands together. "I'm not married as you well know. Do not tell me there is no other way." He expelled a long breath, trying to regain control. Staring out to sea, he strained to see the object drifting near, but nothing broke the calm surface. Gentle waves lapped against the hull.

"You could always get married," Philip suggested.

Tristan turned and raised a brow at him. "Isn't it rather late for that?"

Philip shrugged. "As you've said, you are leagues away from London. No one of consequence could account for the last year of your life. Who's to say you weren't married when we arrived at Port Rìgh."

Tristan shook his head. "I see where you're going with this but let us hurry to the part where we dismiss your idea. If I knew a woman I wished to marry, I would have done so already. Anyway, you know my mind on marriage. I am a man of the sea."

Philip crossed his arms over his chest. "Marrying anyone else would be better than Abigail Roxwell. I heard she had her serving maid flogged for plucking her eyebrows too thin."

Tristan groaned and bent forward, letting his forehead rest on the rail. "I agree with your logic, but I refuse to be forced into one marriage to escape another." Damn Owen and his stubborn hypocrisy. Tristan stood straight and raked his hand through his hair. "It astounds me that my father can be so sensible in every other regard but his ambition to elevate his family to nobility. He cannot see his own folly."

"Mayhap, there is another way," Philip murmured.

Tristan watched his quarter master slowly pace the forecastle. "Yes, indeed, it just might work."

"What are you mumbling about?" Tristan said impatiently.

Philip whirled around, his eyes gleaming. "You could falsify a wedding."

Had his quarter master gone daft? "What are you talking about? Falsify a wedding? What is that supposed to even mean?"

A slight smile curved Philips lips. "Yes!" he said, clearly approving his own plan before Tristan even understood it.

"Don't you see?" Philip blurted, his face now flushed with excitement.

"No, I don't see," Tristan snapped. "I don't know what the hell you're talking about."

Philip grinned. "You could feign being married to someone."

Tristan slowly shook his head. He couldn't believe what Philip had just proposed. "You've lost your mind, old friend."

"Do not dismiss my idea so quickly, not until you consider it from all angles."

"Correct me if I'm wrong, but you are proposing I pretend to have a wife. From every angle that is lunacy."

Philip shrugged. "Desperate times."

Tristan raised his eyes heavenward. "The notion of a fake bride is ridiculous, not to mention blasphemous."

"No," Philip snapped. "You marrying Lady Roxwell is ridiculous, not to mention abhorrent, immoral, unthinkable—"

"Enough," Tristan snapped. It pained him that Philip did not exaggerate. By all accounts, Abigail was entirely lacking in merit, which was no surprise to Tristan. He had witnessed precious little nobility among the noble class.

"There must be another way." He looked out to sea. "Give me the answer," he prayed aloud.

Philip moved to stand next to him. "Pray to the sea all you like, but the more I think on it, the more I am certain marital pretense is the answer."

He scowled at Philip, then turned back to the sea and added to his prayer. "And find me a new quarter master."

Philip flashed a wide grin. "You say that now, but once you think on it, you'll realize my genius." A moment later, Philip's smile faded, and his countenance grew serious. "Tristan, this truly could be the only way to save your family and yourself. It is a simple enough plan. All you need is a woman."

Tristan made a show of looking around the deck at the rough-speaking, weathered sailors, moving about their duties. "And where exactly am I going to find a woman?" he asked.

"Captain," Nelson called down.

Tristan turned and looked to the top of the wide, square mast. "Aye, Nelson. What do you see?"

"Not sure, Captain," came his reply. "But...but I think it could be...a woman."

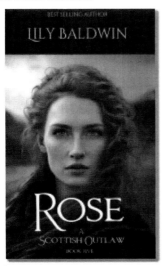

Tristan and Philip locked eyes. Both men stood frozen. Then, a slow smile spread across Philip's face. "It looks like the sea has answered your prayer after all, Captain."

Find your copy of Rose: A Scottish Outlaw, Book Five at Amazon.com.

Wishing you happy reading and many blessings.

All my best,

Lily Baldwin

Made in United States
North Haven, CT
19 June 2023